SMOKEJUMPER

A Summer in the American Wilderness

SMOKEJUMPER

A Summer in the American Wilderness

By Dale L. Schmaljohn

Illustration by
Carl Brown

HYDE PARK PRESS

iv

FOREWORD

The events related in this book are based on my experiences as a smokejumper. The historical, geographical and technical information presented here is accurate; however, the characters are fictitious. I have also changed the locations and time sequence to make them suitable to the story.

For some time I have felt a need to share this story. I hope it is entertaining and generates some thoughts about personal growth. I will feel rewarded if it provides a realistic understanding of smokejumping, reflects favorably on my native state of Idaho, and pays tribute to the free spirit of my smokejumper friends, living and dead.

ACKNOWLEDGEMENTS

I want to thank my friend Carl Brown for contributing all but one of the illustrations for this book, and I am grateful to Bob Auth for allowing me to use his drawing of Buckskin Bill.

CONTENTS

PAYETTE NATI

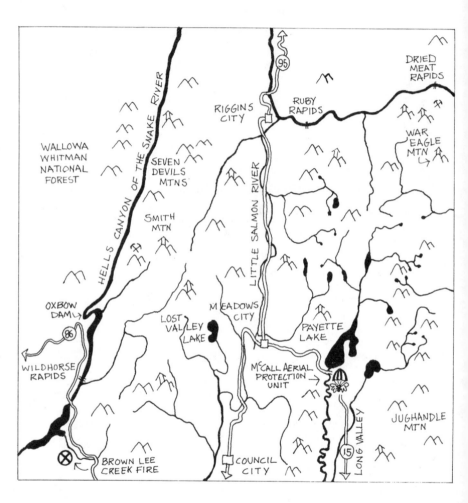

0   5   10 MILES

🌲 FIRE LOOKOUTS   ☐ CITIES   ⚒ GOLD AND SILVER MINES   ⸜ PRIMITIVE AREA BOUNDARY

ᨆ MAJOR MOUNTAINS   ⑨⑤ HIGHWAYS   ✦ RAPIDS AND WATERFALLS

viii

ONAL FOREST

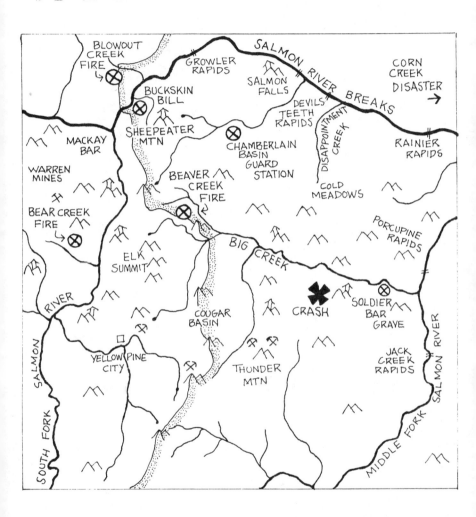

SMOKEJUMPERS
REGION
FOUR

ix

For my sons Pat and Scott.

I wish you the spirit of the Sheepeaters.

1

IN FLIGHT

The drone of the twin engines rose and fell rhythmically as the DC-3 aircraft pulled steadily through the late afternoon sky. The small window revealed the green timbered carpet below, interrupted occasionally by cliffs and granite peaks. The wide expanse of one of the last primitive areas in the United States stretched as far as Scott Patrick's eyes could see. This was the historic land of the Sheepeater Indians, and no sign of mechanized man disturbed the serenity of the Idaho forest below.

A few short months ago this now familiar country was unknown to Scott. Today this beautiful wilderness held him in its spell.

Three months ago the men in this crowded DC-3 were strangers to Scott. Now he shared a kinship with them that had been welded by fire.

Scott felt a bond with this land and the smokejumpers around him. For this had been a summer of change for Scott. His life would never be the same.

Scott listened to the airplane, looked out the window, and remembered how this summer of adventure began................

2

NEDDY NEWMAN

The sign on the hangar read, "Elevation 5021 ft.," on the other side of the highway another sign proclaimed, "Welcome to McCall, Idaho, Ski-land, USA." Scott drove through the small town perched on the shores of beautiful Payette Lake, which stretched north for several miles. Seeing a service station he pulled in.

"So you're a smokejumper?" the attendant said in response to Scott's request for directions.

"Well, I start training in the morning," Scott answered.

"You're about there," the friendly Idahoan said, smiling and wiping his hands on a grease rag. "Stay on the main drag about a quarter of a mile. Let's see, take the second street to your left. Watch to your right and you can't miss it."

Forking over a five dollar bill for the gas, Scott's eyes studied the lake. "Beautiful country around here," he said.

"I've never seen anything nicer," the attendant stated proudly.

"Thanks for the directions," Scott said, starting his car.

"Thank you, and good luck with jump training. I've heard it's a real bear," the young man answered with small town warmth! "See you around."

"See ya," Scott said.

SMOKEJUMPER

"Payette Forest Aerial Protection Unit," announced a stately sign from the center of a manicured lawn. Behind the sign. Scott saw the main building which housed the parachute loft in the two-story, center section. On the outside of the loft was a picture showing Smokey the Bear, descending in a white and orange parachute. Smokey looked comical, Scott smiled as he pulled into the driveway.

Walking to the front door of the deserted building Scott read the notice on the glass:

ATTENTION: New smokejumpers welcome. Your name is on a bed in the north barracks. The locker beside it is yours. Returning jumpers will be in the remaining quarters. Breakfast at 0700. Report to the loft building at 0800 Monday, June 5. Be prepared for your physical fitness test.

A list of twelve names followed. Scott could hardly believe the months of anticipation were over, and he felt pride and excitement when he found his name, Scott Patrick, boldly typed on the list.

He looked for the barracks in the growing darkness, saw lights through the evergreen trees and followed the path toward them.

After the chill of the evening air, the warmth of the building was welcomed.

"Hi, want some help?" a young man said, as he put down his magazine and reached for a box Scott hugged between his arm and side. Freed of the box Scott sat his two suitcases on the floor.

"I'm Scott Patrick," he said extending his hand.

"I'm Guy Edwards," the young man answered dropping the

On the loft building was a picture of Smokey the Bear descending in a bright white and orange parachute.

4

box to an empty cot and shaking Scott's hand. "Have you driven far?" he asked, re-establishing himself in front of the old Spark oil heater.

"From the coast," Scott answered. "Twelve hours, it feels good to be here," he added, stretching.

"Tex Gardner here." The voice startled Scott from behind.

"Didn't even see you when I came in," Scott said apologizing.

"I'm easy to overlook," Tex said with a drawl, shaking Scott's hand firmly. Tex dropped back to his bed and pulled a jacket over his chest. "This darn country's cold," he added. "It's hard to believe we'll soon be having forest fires around here."

"It warms up fast when summer finally gets here," Guy said.

"You guys interested in shooting a game of pool or going to town?" Tex asked from his prone position on the bed.

"Thanks, but I'm tired. I'm going to unpack and crash," Scott answered.

"I'm settled in for the night too," Guy said.

A smiling round face with a head of curly brown hair protruded from the bathroom door. "Another Ned, eh?" he said.

"Ralph Meyers this is Scott Patrick," Guy introduced Scott informally.

"Ned," Scott questioned, confusion showing on his face.

"That's what they call all the rooky smokejumpers here at McCall," Tex said, rolling over on his bed. "No one seems to know how it got started, but Ned is short for Neddy Newman."

Scott unpacked and moved his clothes into the wall locker next to his bed and stood a picture up inside the locker. "I go to the University of Idaho," Guy volunteered. "I've worked on a district fire crew out of McCall for the past three summers."

5

Just then Ralph approached, "Hey, she's cute," he observed, as he stood looking over Scott's shoulder. His large towel wrapped body still pink from the shower. "What's her name?"

"Julie," Scott answered smiling into the picture.

"Ralph knows his women. You should see the pictures he has in his locker," Guy said.

"Yep, Ralph's our barracks' Romeo," Tex added.

"I'll bet," Scott said with doubt in his voice.

"No joke, if you ever need a date, ole Ralphy can fix you up." Ralph grinned devilishly.

"How much do you charge for the use of your little black book? I want a date that likes to shoot pool," Tex asked.

"Shoot pool! Who wants to shoot pool?" said a tall blond-headed guy closing the door behind him.

"I do," Tex answered.

"Well then, let's go," he said turning back to the door.

"Before we take off, Neil, meet Scott Patrick, another Ned." Tex said as he pulled on a jacket.

"Welcome," the blond said, "I'm Neil Prisbee."

"Hi," Scott said shaking his hand, "See you later."

"Don't stay out too late," Ralph warned. "Training starts early and it is going to be tough."

"Sure, Mom," Tex said laughing as he went out the door.

"Are you nervous about training?" Guy said, after Tex and Neil had left.

"Nervous? Yes, but I've spent the last three summers fighting range fires just for the chance to learn to smokejump," Ralph said, "and I plan to make it through."

"Me, too," Guy added. "My brother was a jumper and I

always figured that one day I would do it, too."

"I saw a smokejumper movie on TV when I was in high school, and I've wanted to try it ever since," Scott confessed. "I've worked two summers with a Forest Service crew in northern California."

Scott settled into bed and quickly drifted into a light sleep. He heard the pool players and others return and quietly seek out their cots, as his sleep deepened.

Suddenly all the lights were snapped on. Scott felt his cot lift and overturn. The floor was cold against his bare back. As Scott pushed the mattress aside a loud voice shattered the air and echoed off the barracks' walls.

"On your feet, Neds," ordered a tall, stout figure, his voice as commanding as an army sergeant. A couple of shorter figures stood behind him, dressed as he was, in work shirts, Levis, and heavy logging boots. The three men had worked fast to dump a dozen beds so quickly.

"Give me twenty-five!" ordered the drill sergeant voice, "Push-ups, you thick-headed N-E-D-S! Get started!"

The new recruits realized that being called a Ned was not meant as a compliment as they groggily started the push-ups.

The commander and his raiders watched and laughed in malicious delight.

"You Neds can't keep your barracks clean," the voice barked. "Pick up this mess!" Satisfied with their midnight raid, the three ambled to their own barracks. The rest of the night progressed with a succession of other celebrating "old-timers" wandering through the Neds' barracks raising as much havoc as the first group.

SMOKEJUMPER

Morning finally arrived. The Neds realized that a group identity was already being formed, as they joined the old-timers, who gathered behind the loft building. Standing awkwardly to one side, they looked every bit the new recruits they were. The returning jumpers milled about greeting each other, looking like a rowdy gang of playful boys. Blue jeans and heavy logging boots were standard dress, but shirts and head gear presented some variation in uniform.

Don Lent, the smokejumper foreman, appeared on the platform outside the back door of the loft. A smile creased his weathered face, "Welcome! and Welcome back! I want the new men to stay here. Returning jumpers will meet in the recreation room." The veteran jumpers left; leaving the Neds waiting nervously. A man in his thirties stepped onto the platform as Don turned and went inside. He was of average height with broad shoulders and heavily muscled arms. He had a short, massive neck, and a protruding nose that supported thick glasses. Brown hair showed beneath his weathered baseball cap.

"That's a fifty-jump pin," Guy whispered, referring to the small blue pin on the front of his cap. "My name is Ken Satterfield, for the next three weeks I'll be Uncle Ken to you Neds. Let's hear your morning greeting for Uncle Ken," he said with a broad smile.

"Good morning, Uncle Ken," a few voices answered.

"Give me twenty-five!" Ken's voice boomed back.

Everyone dropped to a lean and rest position and proceeded through twenty-five push-ups as Uncle Ken counted them out slowly—1, 2, 3...

"Now, let's put a little spirit in your good morning!" Ken demanded.

This time the group roared out with all the enthusiasm and formal unison of a well-disciplined first grade class, "GOOD MORNING, UNCLE KEN!"

"Better! Mucho better! Since the job of making you guys into smokejumpers has been given to Chuck and me, I want to assure you that we take our work seriously," Ken said as he pointed to the man next to him.

Chuck was lean and wiry with a blond moustache and hair the color of sun-bleached straw. His face was handsome except for the scars around his right eye and down the side of his throat. Scott's eyes followed the scar down Chuck's right arm and saw that two fingers were missing on his right hand.

"It's not polite to stare at a disabled veteran," Chuck said in a raspy voice. "These are a few souvenirs from Southeast Asia. My voice is another. You'll have to listen up when I'm talking, because I don't have much volume." There was no self-pity in Chuck's voice. In fact, Scott detected a sense of fun in his blue eyes.

"First thing we've got to do is the physical fitness test," Ken said in a clear voice. "You need a minimum amount of strength and conditioning for your own safety and the safety of your fellow jumpers."

Anxiety filled the air as the Neds moved toward the chin-up bar. Scott hoped the excitement surging through him would result in added strength, not in disabling weakness. Chuck's raspy voice counted five pull-ups, but said nothing as Scott's chin rose above the pipe for the sixth time.

"You didn't fully extend your arms on that last one," Chuck answered the questioning look. Struggling now for every pull-up that followed, Scott reached nine and dropped from the bar.

Breathing deeply and trying to recover between the demands of each physical task, Scott moved from station to station with the other men. Finally he stood before the rope climb with its four parallel ropes hanging from a log frame.

As Ralph inched halfway up the rope and hung with limp arms, Chuck's forced voice yelled, "OK, use your feet, but get to climbing!" Then Chuck began to laugh as he looked up at Ralph's large backside, "You look like a giant pear hanging on a tree. Get down from there before you hurt yourself, Ned Bartlett."

"Hey, Ken, show these guys how to climb a rope," Chuck's gravelly voice requested.

Ken sat on the ground with his feet extended straight out in front of him. Effortlessly he sped the 20 feet, then returned to the ground; while never once letting his legs drop from their horizontal position.

"Four seconds, Ken! You're getting old," Chuck heckled.

The new men, impressed and humbled, each struggled with the challenge of the rope climb. Only later did they learn that Ken had been a competition rope-climber in college.

Many of the test scores were averaged to determine whether the Ned was in good enough shape to start training. For example, if he did well in the chin-ups but only fair in sit-ups, his average score could still give him a passing grade. Some tests, however, were scored alone and they had to be passed. One such test was the mile-and-a-half run, and this last challenge would complete Scott's physical fitness tests.

"A mile and a half in eleven minutes shouldn't be too hard," Scott whispered, leaning close to Guy's ear. "I've run it faster than that nearly every day all spring."

"But remember, McCall's elevation is a mile high, and that can make a lot of difference," Guy said.

Scott moved to the starting line painted on the road. "So much depends on this run. If my time is too slow, smokejumper training will be over for me. I've got to relax!" Scott's knees felt weak.

"Go!" Ken called, and Scott lunged forward, hoping to set a pace he could hold.

One of the Neds shot ahead. Neil and Tex were close behind him. Scott tuned in on his own heavy breathing and worried, "Will I even be able to finish the run?"

3

TRAINING: YOU HIRED ON

TO BE TOUGH

After half an hour of calisthenics the Neds moved downstairs to the cool classroom of the loft building; Scott felt relieved to have yesterday's physical fitness test over. He had met his first challenge and even completed the run successfully.

"Did you notice there were only eleven of us?" Guy whispered.

"Who is missing?" Scott asked.

"Remember the guy who won the mile-and-a-half run? He wasn't able to pass enough of the other tests to qualify," Guy said.

"That'd be a bummer." Scott said sympathetically.

"You know it," Guy added.

On the table in front of each Ned lay a long snap with a button release and an odd-looking metal connector about two inches square. Ken began to explain, "The two connectors in front of you are of life and death importance. Get familiar with them and learn to call them by their names." Holding up the long snap, he continued, "This is a static-line snap. You hook it

12

to the cable in the airplane; it is what causes the parachute to open."

"A rather handy device," Chuck added with a smile.

Ken held up the second connector. "This is a capewell. It holds the parachute to your harness." His eyes twinkled behind his thick glasses. "No summer wardrobe is complete without it." Nervous laughter spread through the class.

A dummy dressed in a smokejumper outfit stood silently by as Ken proceeded to describe the protective features of the jumpsuit.

"This is a standard football helmet. The face protector on the front is custom-made."

He pointed out that the jumper's back, ribs and shoulders were padded. Then he showed how the collar on the jacket came up in front of the chin and sloped three-fourths of the way up the back of the helmet.

"Why does it have such a high collar?" asked Neil Prisbee, who sat next to Scott. "Is it just for looks?"

"Yeah, Pretty Boy, just for looks and to keep branches and parachute lines from burning the hair off the back of your neck," Ken answered with a smile. He moved on, pointing out the padded pants and the quick-release zippers down both legs.

"We have your suits out on the lawn and as you try them on, we'll check to see that they fit," Chuck directed.

Seeing the dummy hadn't given Scott any idea of how hot and unnatural the jumpsuits were. The dummy's painted-on smile and straight position had failed to warn him that the buckles would dig into his back and the harness would pull at his shoulders.

13

"How do you expect me to walk in this thing?" Scott asked. "It feels like my knees and shoulders are tied together."

"A perfect fit," Ken said. "Stow your gear, catch some lunch and I'll see you on the training field at 1300 hours," Ken directed. Scott struggled out of his jumpsuit and headed for the fire cache, the building where all the firefighting supplies are kept. Scott stowed his newly awarded jumpsuit in the bin marked "Patrick" and started off for lunch.

After lunch, the Neds waited with their bagged-up jump gear.

"See Uncle Ken over there," Chuck said in his gravelly voice, pointing to Ken some 300 yards away. "Haul your buns over there as fast as you can!"

"Put on your jumpsuits," Ken's voice welcomed their arrival, and he started his stopwatch.

"That took fifteen minutes. You'll have to do better than that if you're going to be part of this outfit," Ken said once they were all suited. "Take off your suits, sack them up and give me twenty-five. Staying with this unit means you have to get to the airport, suit up and be in the air in the time it has taken you just to suit up."

Following the push-ups Ken and Chuck were joined by two assistants, and suiting up practice began in earnest. It would take a week for these trainees to conquer the heavy snaps and zippers and learn to feel when the harness straps were straight.

Next came a lesson on landing rolls. Ken demonstrated as Chuck explained, "Feet together, knees flexed, hop, pivot, shoulder roll, kick." It looked easy when Ken did it, only after hours of practice did it become as natural to them as an inborn reflex.

"Until this roll can be done without thinking, you won't be ready to jump from an airplane," Ken said. From a standing position, from the ramp, swinging from the roll trainer, with jumpsuits off, jumpsuits on—over and over they practiced the landing roll.

"The roll is the thing," Chuck said. "If you can't do it right, you'll get hurt."

"Sack up your gear and hustle over to the jump tower," Chuck's rough voice commanded.

"Hustle!" Scott thought to himself. "Where could I get any more hustle?"

"This jump tower is thirty-two feet high," Ken said. "This height is what the army found to be the psychological breaking point. Anyone who can jump from thirty-two feet can jump from an airplane, or so they say."

Scott stood apprehensively at the base of the tower watching Ken prepare the first man for his jump.

"Yell your name as you step off the tower, just as you will when you jump from an airplane," Ken instructed. "If you run out of wind before you feel your parachute open you had better be reaching for the ripcord on your reserve chute.".

Chuck, who was positioned at the bottom of the tower with a clipboard, would grade the men as they jumped. He checked on each important part of their performance. Were the jumper's feet together? Was his body straight up and down? Did he look toward the horizon as he fell? And did he quickly look up to check the imaginary parachute once he felt the jerk of the rope?

With each step up the stairs, Scott's hands tightly gripped the rail, and his shoulders bent closer to the steps. He felt awkward and clumsy in his jumpsuit and harness. From the ground the tower hadn't looked high, but from the top it was frightening! Slowly, cautiously, Scott took the last two steps. Quietly he stood to one side and raised his head to look around. What a beautiful, breathtaking view! Looking through the clear air, the mountains seemed close enough to reach out and touch. Then, Chuck's voice broke Scott's daydream and fear returned in a flash.

Scott could hear Ken's instructions to the man in front of him. The Ned made all the necessary preparations for his exit, but then he stepped back and turned around. Scott saw that it was Fred, a quiet fellow bunking two beds down from him. Fred stood talking quietly to Ken and shaking his head. Slowly Fred unsnapped the capewells that held his harness to the rope mechanism and moved to one side.

Ken motioned for Scott to move into position, and Fred started back down the stairs. Stepping forward, Scott's heart pounded in his ears. He was suddenly aware of the possibility that he might not be able to jump off the tower. Up to this point he had been too busy to think of this giant step that awaited him. Trying to control his fear Scott listened to Ken's voice. His anxiety made Ken's briefing hard to follow, and his hands jerked as he tightened the straps on his parachute harness.

"Are you ready?" Ken asked.

"Yes," Scott said, standing squarely in the door, eyes on the horizon, muscles tensed.

16

"Are you sure?" Ken asked again.

"Yes," Scott barked, wanting to get it over and done with.

Something crashed against Scott's helmet.

He opened his eyes to see Ken's arm reached across the door in front of him. In Ken's right hand dangled the part of the cape-well that should have been connected to Scott's harness; Ken had hit Scott's helmet with it. Had Scott stepped off the tower, he would have fallen thirty-two feet to the safety net below. His mouth and throat went dry making it hard to swallow as he realized the seriousness of his oversight.

"I hope you all saw that," Ken shouted to the others. "You have got to think all the time in this business, especially when you're scared!" he scolded: "Now if Mrs. Patrick's little boy, Scotty, will pay attention we'll get on with training," Ken said, looking sternly at Scott.

Still the step off the tower awaited him. Mustering all his courage and checking his hook-up carefully, Scott again awaited Ken's slap on his leg.

This time the slap came and with his eyes tightly shut, Scott hurled himself through the door. Scott then remembered — eyes on the horizon, feet together, he began yelling "P-a-t-r-i-c-k" and it was over. He had just completed his first tower jump and relief flooded his tired body. Hanging above the safety net, Scott looked at Chuck and saw him point up. Oh yes, he had even forgotten to make the simulated check of his parachute. "That jump just killed you," Chuck said grimly

For ten Neds, jumping off the tower grew easier and seemed less complex with practice. Like a well-rehearsed football play, exiting from the tower soon became automatic. Fred, who didn't jump from the tower that day, was given some time to see how he would deal with his fear. Every other Ned knew that Fred was going to have a tough decision to make, and no one gave him any trouble as he quietly struggled within himself.

In the wooden airplanes, called mock-ups, the Neds practiced take-off procedures, rehearsed exiting the plane and learned to drop cargo.

Chuck was role-playing the part of the spotter. After a simulated check of the wind, he checked each would-be jumper's equipment carefully. Scott would be the first smokejumper to exit the mock plane. He attached the static-line of his parachute to a cable running the length of the mock-up. "Once your chute opens, face in the direction of the plane.........," Chuck spoke directions into the earhole of Scott's helmet as if this role-play were a real fire jump. Scott braced himself in the open doorway and Chuck lay on his stomach, looking out the door. Chuck pulled his head up quickly, slapped the back of Scott's leg and yelled, "GO! GO!" and Scott stepped from the mock-up with the same cautious procedure used to exit the jump tower, but this time he was only a couple of feet above the ground.

At times Ken, in his good-natured way, stood toward the front of the wooden plane, roaring his deep voice, simulating the sound of the engines. At other times Chuck and Ken pretended to be stewardesses on the plane.

"Coffee, tea, or me," Ken joked in a high, strained voice.

Despite the humor, Scott found his body tense and his heart

racing each time he rehearsed the jump procedure.

Smokejumpers sometimes land in trees, so it is important that they know how to get down safely. The procedure for this is called a "let-down" and practicing it was the next training adventure. The Neds pulled themselves twenty feet into the air with a pulley system and performed the maneuver while their trainers timed them with stopwatches. Although the procedure was simple, it had to be done precisely. The letdown training proved to be fun even in the hot jumpsuits.

"Look at Mrs. Edward's little boy, Guy, with all his blood rushing to his head," teased Chuck as he pointed to Guy hanging upside down from the let-down trainer.

The Neds laughed nervously as Guy kicked and struggled to free himself. It was funny for a while, but Scott got angry as he watched his friend struggle helplessly. Ken finally untied the rope on the pulley and slowly lowered Guy to the ground.

"Had this been for real," Chuck said seriously, "there would be absolutely no way anyone could have helped Edwards down from a tall tree. This has been a tough lesson for Guy, but I hope you all learned it!"

Scott realized that the day would come when they would all be thankful that Ken and Chuck had insisted that they learn to do things properly in an alert, flexible manner. Guy's mistake, like Scott's on the jump tower, was of value to everyone.

After a rest session with the trainers answering questions, rolls were practiced again, and again, and again.

"The obstacle course is only a quarter of a mile long. It can't be too bad," Scott whispered to Tex as the last challenge of the day approached. But when Scott's turn came and he was struggling over the eight-foot wall, he realized that a quarter of a mile could be a long way. Scott knew the obstacle course had been well-named, as he hopped through the cross-bucks, cleared the hurdles, walked arm over arm across the overhead ladder, leap-frogged the truck tires, panted through the culvert, and stumbled through the brush to the finish line.

The trainers now gave these new recruits time to rest and regain their wind before they finished the day as they had started it, with a few minutes of calisthenics.

Having finished the exercises, Ken said, "See you in back of the parachute loft at 0800 tomorrow. We'll really get going then." A tired groan went up from eleven weary Neds.

Looking surprised at their protest, Ken made what would become a familiar statement: "Remember folks, you hired on to be tough."

With his, eleven sore and exhausted bodies quietly moved toward the barracks.

4

GETTING BETTER EVERY DAY

By 0800, Scott and the others stood on the training field awaiting their second day of smokejumper training. The Neds had made a serious-looking group as they hobbled down the hill to breakfast. Now they stood quietly with the pain and stiffness of men three times their age.

"Was it the shock of being jerked by the jump tower, or could it have been the endless jarring of practice landings that is making me ache all over?" Scott thought to himself. He realized the physical exercise alone couldn't result in such torment.

"GOOD MORNING, UNCLE KEN!" The Neds bellowed out with all the strength they could muster. They hoped that enough enthusiasm would prevent an untimely twenty-five push-ups.

"Good morning, Neddies," Ken returned their greeting as he smiled from ear to ear.

"We can't train your bodies and overlook your minds in this day of concern for the whole person," Ken added. "So we're going to add a little saying to our morning greeting. It goes like this: 'I'm getting better every day, I'm getting better in every way.' Now let's hear it."

"I'M GETTING BETTER EVERY DAY, I'M GETTING

BETTER IN EVERY WAY," the Neds responded with volume and enthusiasm, even if a coordinated effort was lacking.

"Twenty-five," Ken ordered and his Neds dropped to their now familiar position to await his count. When they were again on their feet, Ken said, "Let's try it one more time."

"I'M GETTING BETTER EVERY DAY, I'M GETTING BETTER IN EVERY WAY," the Neds roared with the unison of a choral group.

"Beautiful!" Ken said with a self-satisfied smile. "Let's loosen up a bit."

Thus, a new ritual had been added to the schedule.

With Ken leading the way, morning exercises began. The stiff, sore muscle fibers began to crack and loosen. To Scott's surprise, in a matter of minutes his body began to respond smoothly. Spirit began to return to the group, and power and enthusiasm grew as they shouted out the count of the exercises. With arms extended straight out from their bodies and their hands rotating in small circles, they made the roaring sound of a DC-3 airplane. When their arms were extended over their heads, the slapping sound of a helicopter rotor was expected. On other exercises the Neds snarled and growled as instructed. It was evident that these experienced trainers knew how to instill morale and esprit de corps. Exercises ended with a mile run, and then off to the classroom for the rest of the morning.

The classes taught techniques for controlling forest fires, and how to monitor lightning fires on National Park or other specially designated lands where a natural ecology is maintained. There was so much to learn: how the parachute functions, first aid, and, of course, how to fill out fire reports. The list went on and on, enough to fill the mornings for two weeks.

The afternoons were much the same as the first one, with more expected each day as smoothness and rhythm began to appear. The fledglings continued to work hard at mastering the many and varied skills needed in their new profession.

The old-timers now left the Neds alone; there was no more harassment such as they had experienced the first night after they had arrived. Scott had often heard Ken say, "What is fair is fair," and the other old-timers must have believed this, too, for their nights were left free to get the sleep they so badly needed.

The jump tower convinced Fred that he didn't like the heights involved in smokejumping, and at the end of the second day he decided to return to the lookout position he had held during previous summers. Smokejumping was not for him. That left ten Neds.

"How many and who will be left by the end of training?" Scott wondered. The Neds had formed a close group and they worked hard to help each other get through their individual rough spots. Ralph had the most trouble, and he was continually encouraged and cheered on by the others.

The new smokejumpers were now doing landing rolls from the back of a pickup truck as it sped around the training field. With the added speed, Scott felt his mistakes and listened with his ears wide open when Ken or Chuck explained how to correct them. No one had to tell Scott to remember to tuck his head; if he forgot, stars danced before his eyes.

"Pretty Boy, keep those hands up; don't drop them when you're landing," Ken shouted at Neil Prisbee for the tenth time. "Take five!" Ken said over his shoulder as he started toward the back door of the parachute loft. In a couple of minutes he returned with the loft foreman, Wayne Garrison, who Scott remembered from his previous demonstration of parachute packing.

Wayne was a tall, distinguished-looking man. He had smokejumped for many years. Now his main job was to supervise the care of all chutes and equipment. Yet, like an old fire horse, he jumped on fires whenever he got the chance. His appearance demanded respect as he moved toward the suited men.

"Wayne has something to show you folks, especially you, Pretty Boy." Ken said.

Wayne took off his shirt, revealing a wide white scar that ran at an angle from his upper forearm to the base of his neck.

"This is what you get if you drop your hands when you're landing in rocks," Wayne informed them as he moved his arm up so that it was pointing straight out from his shoulder.

He continued to raise it to this height several times as he said, "Before I injured this arm I could raise it straight over my head—like this." As he said, "Like this," his arm shot up high and straight, well above his head. He began to laugh as he looked into the Neds' surprised faces. They joined in Wayne's laughter once they recovered from the surprise of seeing his "critically" injured arm moving freely.

"Seriously," Wayne said. "I did dislocate this arm by dropping my hands too quickly one time when I parachuted into a rock pile, and it has taken a lot of work and pain to get the use of it back." Still chuckling, Wayne strode toward the loft building and the crew again loaded into the back of the pickup.

24

The days faded together and what had seemed to be an overwhelming amount to learn somehow seemed to be falling into place. Then, one afternoon the end of ground training came for Scott and the other Neds. As they removed their jumpsuits, their shirts and Levis were soaked with sweat as usual. Scott vividly recalled Chuck's words the first day when he handed him his suit. "You'll find that the best thing about this is taking it off."

Scott stuffed his jumpsuit almost ritualistically into the gear bag. The remainder of the afternoon would be spent going one at a time before the training review board, where the trainers and Don Lent would review each candidate's readiness to move to the next stage of smokejumper training—making practice jumps from an airplane.

"Will this be the end of my smokejumper career, or will I actually be parachuting from an airplane in two days?" Scott asked himself. He felt little comfort with either possibility.

5

CEREMONIES AND

PARACHUTING

Scott finished his letter to Julie and continued to think about her as he sat back in his chair looking at her picture.

Two welcome days of rest had passed quickly, and now Scott awaited his first training jump in the morning. It reassured him to know that all ten Neds had been cleared to make this jump.

Scott was restless and had slept only fitfully. The last time he checked his watch, it was two o'clock. The barracks were quiet. Scott hoped the traditional initiation has been forgotten. He tried to relax and force the thought of tomorrow from his mind; he knew that the dark of night was no time to think about his first parachute jump.

A strange sound broke the silence. It came again. Startled, Scott sat upright in bed. The sound came once more, low at first, then steadily increasing in volume. It was a chanting of many voices. Low, mournful, death-like moans were frequently pierced with a yapping noise like that of a coyote. Scott tried hard to clear his mind, but dreams and reality tended to merge.

The door opened slowly and Scott knew it was not a dream. The old-timers were up to no good. But he couldn't recognize

26

anyone — they were all draped in white bed sheets which formed hoods over their heads and they held flashlights to cast morbid shadows across their faces. It all seemed so ridiculously weird that Scott couldn't hold back his laughter.

"Do — not — laugh," a stern voice ordered, as the ghosts moved in close around the laughing Ned. "Lie out on the floor, Ned Patrick," the voice directed. The others let forth with loud moans and screams. Not questioning the authority in the voice, the now sober Ned followed orders, and lay shivering on the cold floor. A paper cross was placed on his chest and the ghostly forms poured cold liquid over his shivering body. At the voice's command, Ned Patrick sat up. He was given a drink of foul-tasting fluid, and half gagging, he swallowed. The voices moaned out that this was embalming fluid. Scott shook with cold and anxiety and he didn't laugh again. He began to accept the craziness of the situation as reality just as he saw those around him doing. Then he lay on his bunk as the spooky figures moved to Ralph's bed.

"On the floor Ned Myers," commanded a cloaked voice. The round body went prone on the floor. The tiles against his bare back caused him to shake with the cold.

"Neddy, with the body of a Bartlett pear, take a drink," a deep voice said. He held the bottle ritualistically as Ralph drank. One ghost held an artificial leg above his hooded head, another waved a crutch as he moaned and chanted.

Each Ned in turn paid his dues to the solemn group of "ghosts." Each novice smokejumper was told to draw a card from a deck. When a black card was drawn, the shadowy forms mournfully interpreted it to mean death in the morning. When a red card was drawn, they again moaned loudly, for this too was a bad omen, indicating that horrible injury lay ahead. After an hour of these ghoulish games the strange figures vanished into the night as quickly as they had come.

Through chattering teeth, the Neds laughed with relief and nervousness as they reassured each other that this was just a customary initiation. Following hot showers they tried to salvage some sleep from what remained of the night.

In the morning there was no evidence or mention of the ghostly visitors. Instead, the old-timers enthusiastically wished the new-comers well. The Neds suited up at the airport and prepared to load into the DC-3 that waited to lift them into the air for their first parachute jump.

Scott quickly pulled on his jumpsuit and harness while Tex held the main parachute he would use for his first jump. Bending at the waist, Scott unsnapped the half of the capewell that was attached to the shoulder section of his harness, and Tex placed the parachute on his back much as he would throw a saddle on a horse.

"One," Tex said as he snapped the left capewell closed. "Two," he added, with the softer sound of the safety cover snapping in place to protect the main connection. "One, two," Tex repeated as he hooked up the right capewell. With both capewells fastened, the parachute was soundly attached to Scott's harness. This hook-up procedure was of such importance to the smokejumpers' safety that they were taught to count the four clicks each and every time they helped someone with their parachute. This was the connection Scott had forgotten on the jump tower.

28

SMOKEJUMPER

Scott buckled the waist belt that hung from the parachute.

Tex handed Scott the metal snap attached to the end of the static line, and Scott placed it carefully down the front of his jumpsuit. Here it could be quickly retrieved when he needed to hook-up in the airplane. Next came a smaller, tightly packed reserve parachute that he attached to the front of Scott's harness with four snaps. Should the main parachute malfunction, Scott would have to pull the reserve's shiny silver rip cord. Strapped to the top of this second chute was an eight-inch knife in a protective sheath, strategically placed so that it could be reached should the jumper become entangled in the parachute or encounter some other emergency that required cutting the lines.

Thinking about the possibility of needing the emergency equipment increased Scott's already high level of anxiety.

Sensing the Neds' uneasiness, one of the veteran jumpers slowly sniffed the air in all directions. "Yes, I smell death in the air."

"Don't tell the Neds, we wouldn't want to frighten them," added another old-timer, as he looked serious and stood obviously within voice range. The others looked equally concerned about the Neds' emotional state and agreed that things didn't look good at all.

"They sound a lot like our ghostly friends from last night," Scott whispered in Tex's ear, trying hard not to let them psych him out.

The ten Neds loaded into the DC-3.

The pilot revved the engines as he made the pre-take-off check, and the body of the old aircraft whined from the vibrations. Then, speeding down the runway, it lifted into the air. As the plane gained altitude, Chuck carefully checked each Ned in turn, quietly reassuring them, then moved to the back edge of the door where Ken was sitting. Ken was in his jumpsuit and would be the first one to jump today. From the ground, he would direct each Ned's descent with a megaphone.

Scott turned his attention to the scenery below. He marveled at the breathtaking sight of the small town nestled between the lake on the north and the lush mountain valley on the south. Toy buildings, animals, and cars seemed to be scattered about as in a child's play area. "Looking at the world from this point of view is all right," Scott thought to himself.

Guy interrupted his thoughts, and reminded him that this wasn't a scenic tour when he said, "The lake is calm, looks like the only wind we'll have is up high. A good omen, I would say."

"You're the first guy I've seen in two days that's willing to point out anything but bad omens," Scott said in a weak attempt at humor.

When the plane began to circle above the big open meadow, Scott knew that they had reached the jump area and the proper jump altitude. There would be no trees to worry about today. He watched in fascination as the colorful streamers Chuck released fell silently toward the ground. Chuck followed their fall intently to check the wind direction, and to determine where he would tell the jumpers to leave the plane. Each time the plane passed over the designated jump spot, one man would be signaled to jump. If Chuck failed to direct the pilot over the correct spot, or if he let the jumper out too early or too late, the jumper wouldn't be able to reach the jump spot. Scott was glad Chuck would spot him on this first attempt.

SMOKEJUMPER

Ken stood up, hooked his static-line and took the ready position in the open door. Chuck stood and gave directions into the ear hole of Ken's helmet. The plane banked and slowly straightened out above Big Meadow, as Chuck lay on his stomach near the rear or trailing edge of the door. His headset and goggles protruded out the door and the wind blew his hair back tight against his head. With his left hand, Chuck held a speaker to his mouth; his right hand rested against Ken's logging boot. Scott watched intently as Chuck, in one quick, smooth movement, pulled his head back from the door, slapped the back of Ken's leg and shouted, "GO!"

There was a sound of rushing wind that sent Scott's heart pounding as Ken was swallowed up, leaving no trace of his earlier presence.

Scott's eyes focused on Ken, who hung like a toy paratrooper that had been thrown into the air. Scott felt a rush of fear as he looked at the tiny figure dangling alone, and suddenly he understood why the trainers had worked so hard to teach self-reliance.

Chuck pulled the static-line and empty parachute bag back into the airplane. With each pass over the jump spot he repeated the procedure and dropped another Ned.

Scott looked around the nearly empty plane, suddenly realizing it was his turn. As if in a dream, he hooked his static-line and moved toward the exit position in the open door. He was no longer an observer. He was next! His fear increased with every beat of his heart. He carefully moved through the procedures he had over-learned in countless training rehearsals. Chuck was saying something about a little wind from the north. He told Scott to face the plane after his parachute was open. To look down, Scott leaned forward and felt the crush of the prop blast against his face. His heart pounded wildly as he jerked his head back inside, his eyes blurring from the stinging cold air. Gasping to get the air back that had been sucked from his lungs, Scott clutched the edge of the door with his gloved fingers. He was being pulled toward the open door as if by a giant vacuum cleaner. Every muscle strained against the relentless force.

The slap from Chuck's hand on the back of Scott's leg sent him falling into the rushing, noisy wind. His eyes were shut tight and he held his breath as he tumbled into space. With a snap he was pulled back to a vertical position and there was no roar, no wind, no panic, only quiet. Scott's body hung exhausted beneath the bright orange and white canopy of his parachute.

"How peaceful to be suspended 1500 feet over this big meadow. How comical these little people look standing around their miniature cars," Scott thought, as life poured back into him. He began to revive and drank deeply of the fresh air. Looking down, Scott saw the yellow plastic sheet marking the jump spot. Beautiful, bright parachutes stretched to either side of the yellow plastic.

"I am free," Scott wanted to shout as he turned and swung gently in the air. "What a thrill! It is great to be alive!"

"Wake up, Ned Patrick" Ken's voice shattered the silence from the ground below and brought the giddy Ned sharply back to reality. "Pull your right guideline and come over here with the rest of us," the voice on the megaphone commanded.

Remembering to stay upwind, Scott worked the parachute

first to the right, then to the left, and finally a couple of full turns. As he came closer to the ground the figures below grew into full-sized people.

"What a sensation!" Scott thought to himself. "I'm on top of the world! I can do anything!" Scott was once again high on the thrill of parachuting. He was delighted to be alive.

"Feet together and prepare to land." The instructions from the ground reached him just as the ground slapped him cruelly on the soles of his feet. His knees buckled and he crashed forward. Scott's helmet hit next, and dust flew as he lay stunned. He didn't move for several seconds. Then slowly he struggled to his feet and proceeded to lay out the cloth streamer he carried in the leg pocket of his jumpsuit. Still stunned, Scott placed it in the shape of an "L," indicating to the spotter that he was not injured. Guy helped him gather up his jump gear and pack it over to the truck. Talking excitedly, reliving every detail of their first jump, they watched the remaining Neds descend.

The group of excited Neds grew louder as the stack of jump gear and parachutes rose higher in the back of the truck. Finally ten Neds were telling the stories of their jumps all at once. With steadily growing volume, each tried to get his version heard above his competitors. With the silent wisdom of many smokejumper seasons, Ken patiently waited for the excitement to burn itself out.

Chuck returned to the airport with the pilot. He then took one of the trucks that had been left at the airport and drove to join the Neds at Big Meadow. When Chuck arrived, this group of self-proclaimed heroes had returned to being Neds, with a lot of work to do and many things to learn.

They gathered in a circle around Ken and Chuck to review their day's performance. Each Ned had been evaluated on his exit from the plane, his handling of his parachute, and his landing roll attempt. Chuck described Scott's exit, "It looked like a death-defying leap."

"Ned Patrick, you get a "P" which stands for 'poor' on chute handling, and you earned a double "P" on your landing roll," Ken said as he described Scott's three-point landing: toes, knees, and nose.

Each Ned's performance was reviewed in a similar manner. Quality varied widely, but it was evident that there was a lot of work to be done. Landing rolls would need the most work and Chuck made it clear that the Neds would be doing rolls out of the pickup after lunch. "Tomorrow we'll expect to see some evidence that the time we've spent training you hasn't been wasted," Chuck stated.

"This was about typical for first jumps," Ken added in his reassuring manner. "That's why you have seven practice jumps your first year."

There was a little time before the Neds needed to be back to the smokejumper base for lunch, and Ken suggested that they each tell a little bit about themselves. The previous weeks had been so filled with training that they had learned little about the group's varied backgrounds.

The Neds insisted that Ken be first to tell about himself. He had seemed so natural as a smokejumper and trainer that Scott had never thought about what he did during the winter months. He knew that a few of the older jumpers worked with the Aerial Protection Unit the year around, but most of them were college students, teachers, or worked at other jobs during the winter.

"I'm married and have two children, a boy and a girl," Ken stated. "I'm a junior high school counselor and coach most of the year."

Scott could tell from his voice and enthusiasm that he enjoyed his work. Scott had no trouble seeing the tough, hard trainer as a coach, and the voice that spoke now revealed Ken as an understanding, reachable person, no doubt a good counselor.

"My hobby, or I might say passion, is studying the Indians of central Idaho," Ken continued. "The Sheepeater tribe is especially fascinating to me. What a people! But I don't want to get started talking about them or we won't make it to lunch," Ken's entire body and face reflected his excitement about this subject.

"Sheepeaters? I've never heard of that tribe," Tex questioned.

"Don't get Ken started. He can tell you stories about the Sheepeaters and their chiefs until the snow flies," Chuck warned laughingly.

"I guess I'll be next and get this over with," Chuck said in his gravelly voice. "I'm a graduate of Saigon U," referring to his army days and the scars from his injuries. "I work for the Forest Service the year round. The part I like best is the outside work, but during the cold months I work in the parachute loft repairing chutes and making equipment." Scott could see that talking was a strain on Chuck's injured vocal cords.

In his south western accent Tex began, "I was raised on a small farm in Texas. I guess eventually I will run the farm once my Dad retires. There is only me and my sister. When I was discharged from the paratroopers I decided I needed some time to decompress before I settled down to a farm. That's how I got here," a grin spread across his face as he sighed and leaned back into the trunk of a pine tree.

Scott's plans were different and he willingly told the group that someday he hoped to be a lawyer. He felt just a twinge of longing for his family as he told of growing up in Oregon. "My folks run a hardware store in a little town near the coast. My Dad thinks flying over mountains is dangerous and that jumping out of airplanes is just plain stupid, but my eleven-year-old brother thinks smokejumping is pretty cool." Scott was surprised how freely he talked of his family and future plans. It was as if he were hearing his own voice, but unaware of where it was coming from.

Ken continued around the circle. Teasingly he asked the others what they wanted to be when they grew up.

"When you grow up in New Meadows you're either in the cattle or lumber business," Guy said referring to the little town a few miles west of McCall. "And people who manage to get through college usually teach school or are forest rangers," he said with a smile. "I'm no teacher, so if everything goes well I guess I'll be the Ronnie Ranger type," he added self-consciously.

"We Idahoans have to stick together, seeing as these out-of-state folks keep crowding in on us," Ralph said, his brown curls showing the imprint of his helmet.

"You natives need someone to civilize you and teach you how to kick the horse dung off your boots," a Ned from Southern California said, throwing a pine cone at Ralph's head.

"Like we need a hole in our heads," Ralph fired back, ducking the pine cone.

"I just look at it as a form of missionary work," the Californian answered.

"Speaking of missionary work," Ralph said, "I really do want to be a Lutheran minister should I ever grow up."

"I sure do like your ski country here in Idaho," Neil said. "I'm on the National Ski Patrol and I don't see anything that looks better than smokejumpin' and ski bummin'. At least for awhile." Neil continued explaining that he was a military brat. His father was in the Air Force and his family had lived all over the world.

The sharing continued around the circle. There was no way to know how many of the dreams would ever be realized, but at the moment it was only the sharing that was important.

"How much alike people are, and how rarely we share our sameness," Scott thought.

6

SPILLS AND BROKEN BONES

The Neds continued jumping in the mornings and having class and field training later in the day. The afternoons were relaxed, but full, as the new jumpers developed skills with chain saws, pumps, and other firefighting equipment.

Scott felt that he should be getting over his fear of jumping from planes, but the fear persisted.

The rocking, unsteady plane, the smell of fuel and exhaust, the cold turbulent air boiling past the open door, and, most of all, the relentless roar of the engines made jumping out of airplanes completely unnerving. "It's got to get easier with practice," Scott tried to convince himself. "But will it? How can something continue to be so scary and yet be such a thrilling sensation?" he asked himself.

The third jump was their first experience in timbered terrain. As he looked straight down on the tops of the evergreen trees, Scott's panic level went soaring almost out of control, but with his jaw set and eyes tightly closed, he hurled himself through the open door.

Like the other Neds, Scott managed to land in a tree. He held his breath as the branches rushed past him, striking against his face mask, bending out of the way or breaking under his weight.

SMOKEJUMPER

Scott wasn't sure whether it was the adrenalin pumping through his body or the well-engineered jumpsuit, but he felt no pain as he crashed toward the earth. Then, with a springy jerk, he stopped, his lines tangled in the limbs. Scott looked down cautiously and saw that he had come to a stop high in the tree.

"Should I move," Scott thought to himself, "Or will the slightest movement loosen my chute and send me plummeting to the ground?"

Scott knew that falling from trees was the number one cause of smokejumper injuries. Without moving a muscle, he moved his eyes slowly. His face mask interferred with his vision, but Scott realized that he needed to keep his helmet on in case he should fall. He saw a branch two feet from his right side. S-l-o-w-l-y, slowly, almost holding his breath, Scott raised his right hand and reached for the branch. He almost had it when a "S-N-A-P" sounded high in the yellow pine, and Scott was falling again. His heart wedged in his dry throat, but again he stopped. This time a limb pushed against his left arm.

Scott grabbed with both hands and clung to the limb. Holding his body weight with one hand, he reached above his head and grabbed a handful of parachute lines. With all his strength he jerked, but the lines held firm and Scott knew that the chute was solidly caught in the tree. He could now move freely without worrying that he might crash to the ground. His tense body relaxed as he contemplated his next move.

A picture of Guy hanging helplessly from the let-down trainer flashed in Scott's mind. He thought carefully through the steps of the let-down before beginning. Scott pulled the tie-string at the top of his leg pocket and carefully fed out ten feet of rope.

Then he threaded it through the two D-rings sewed securely to the front of his jump pants, and tied the rope to the parachute lines. Pulling out the slack, Scott tied a slip-knot around the thigh of his left leg and dropped the rope to the ground. He double checked his procedure; he couldn't screw up now. His mouth was dry as cotton as he checked to be sure his gloves were on. He knew he might burn the meat off his fingers if he made a mistake while attempting the let-down without his gloves.

"I'm ready! It's got to be done!" Scott reasoned to himself, as he released the double latch of his right capewell. His body hung awkwardly from the left capewell, and he now fumbled to release it. The full weight of his body drew the rope taut, and he was now ready to release the slip-knot and lower himself to the ground.

Everything went smoothly, but once on the ground, Scott felt exhausted. He began shedding the hot jumpsuit. The cool breeze was heavenly as it blew across his sweat-soaked shirt.

"Did you have fun up there?" Guy's voice greeted Scott.

"You kiddin?" Scott answered. "I saw you decided to try out a tree yourself."

"Oh, I just picked out a little one compared to yours," Guy heckled. "I decided I could use the let-down practice, but I wanted to try it at a safe distance above the ground."

"Sure you did," Scott answered.

"I'll help you get your chute down if you'll help me," Guy offered.

"You're on!" Scott replied. "I can see I've got the best of this deal."

Scott put the climbing spurs on his boots and carefully

proceeded back up the tree. Climbing about the huge yellow pine, Scott learned why smokejumpers don't intentionally choose to land in trees; retrieving a parachute from a tree is a tough job. It is dangerous and just plain old-fashioned hard work. The sweat rolled off Scott as he cautiously moved about, sawing off the limbs that held the parachute lines. The limbs on this tree were ten feet apart in some places, and had it not been for the lineman climbers strapped to his boots, the task would have been impossible. Scott's body quivered from the tension and physical stress of climbing, reaching, and sawing with the short-handled folding saw. His mouth was drier than he had ever remembered as he worked and tried to avoid looking at the ground below. Scott cut through one last limb, and when Guy gave a stout pull on the let-down rope, the parachute fell free.

The only serious accident during the training occurred on the sixth practice jump. The new jumpers were jumping in pairs, one behind the other. This procedure is known as a "two-man stick."

Scott was to be the first man out of the plane on his two-man stick. Balancing in the open door he felt Tex push into him as the plane rocked and bounced on its approach to the jump zone. The helmeted form behind him pressed Scott into the hissing, roaring turbulence rushing past the open door. Scott and Tex stepped free of the plane and their parachutes blossomed to life simultaneously.

"GO RIGHT," Tex yelled and Scott pulled his right guideline. Tex was close, but above Scott and Scott had to trust his judgment if they were to escape a collision. With his heart pounding, Scott held into the right turn making a full 360 degree rotation above Big Meadow.

"LEFT! LEFT!" came the excited cry from above. Scott forced his head back and through the transparent orange parachute he saw a dark silhouette with the sun behind it.

"Turn LEFT! LEFT!" Tex continued to call as he struggled to free himself of Scott's chute. Then, as if in a free fall, Tex dropped like a rock past Scott, his chute flapping above him. Once Tex was below Scott, Scott's chute then collapsed, sending limp parachute lines down around Scott's head and shoulders. Before he could look at the ground to check his speed of descent, he was falling past Tex, whose parachute was now fully opened.

When Scott was lower than Tex the nylon parachute lines tightened suddenly. One line caught under the edge of his helmet pulling his head at an uncomfortable angle. Scott couldn't move his head as he fought to free the line. His right hand fumbled at the knife on his reserve parachute. "How fast am I falling?" Scott thought frantically.

Before Scott could unsheath the eight inch knife, the need for it had passed. His chute again fluttered limply, and he could move his head freely. Scott realized he was again descending past Tex as he brushed the skirt of his taut canopy.

"PULL YOUR RIGHT GUIDELINES," came Ken's voice on the megaphone. Scott and Tex both tried to turn away from each other, but the lines of their chutes would not separate. Scott knew that if they continued this tangled, out-of-control plunge, one of them would be killed! Scott felt his heart sink and his body go weak as the ground rushed up. "This must be a nightmare!" he thought. "It's time to wake up, WAKE UP!" Scott's inner voice screamed.

42

SMOKEJUMPER

"HANG ON TO EACH OTHER," commanded Ken's calm voice from the ground. Tex extended his arms and snagged Scott as gravity again pulled him by. Scott threw both arms around his jump partner's head, and they clung to each other. One parachute lost air completely and fluttered to one side, the other appeared swollen and and strained with its double burden. There was no way to guide the swollen chute, and the pair drifted over the gravel road and landed with a "THUD!"

Tex moaned as Scott stood up and began untangling the mess of parachute lines. "I've hurt my leg," Tex said lying in the tangled chutes. His teeth clinched in pain.

"Don't move," Scott said, trying to appear calm.

Ken pushed his way through the forming group. "Are you guys OK?" he asked.

"It looks like Tex has done something to his leg," Scott answered.

"Let's have a look at it," Ken said kneeling beside Tex. "We had better take him to town," he added after a quick look.

Several Neds lay Tex comfortably in the back of the pickup truck.

"I'll drive him to the hospital," Chuck volunteered as he crawled behind the wheel.

Ken turned to Scott as the pickup pulled away. "Remember how I explained that a parachute forms a partial vacuum above it? When Tex's chute opened it was directly above yours, so it lost air because of the vacuum. He fell through the guide slot in your chute; and then when he dropped below you, that robbed your air. That's the way it went see-sawing all the way down."

Scott's face was pale. "So that was it, ha?" he said weakly.

"Thank God you got hold of each other, or we would be cleaning one of you up with a putty knife," Ken said. "Hope your pal isn't laid up long."

Tex's sun-tanned body contrasted with the white bed sheets and pastel color of the hospital room. "They'll put a walking cast on this in a few days," Tex explained. "Doc feels I may be jumping forest fires by the end of August."

"Good!" Scott said reassuringly. "You can't keep a good man down."

"It's just too bad it had to happen," Guy said regretfully.

"Sometimes you get the bear and sometimes the bear gets you," Tex said resigned to his broken leg.

"At least you won't have to make the pack out tomorrow with the rest of us grunts," Scott added.

"A broken leg! What some people will do to get out of work," Guy said, laughing and shaking his head.

7

FINAL TEST

AND GRADUATION

It was a beautiful, clear McCall morning when the Neds made their last practice jump. All went well. Two Neds landed in trees but everyone else hit in the clearing. This jump was the simulated fire jump, and the jump site was as close as possible to the real thing. The clearing where they landed and the simulated forest fire were on the side of a steep mountain, three and a half miles from McCall. While the jumpers gathered up their gear the plane dropped five bundles of fire-fighting equipment. Saws, shovels, bedrolls, and food rained down in large canvas bags attached to puffy white cargo chutes.

The DC-3 flew low on its cargo pass. "It looks like it is going to fly right into the trees," Scott hollered to Neil over the airplane's roar. Chuck was close enough to be seen clearly as he pushed the bundles from the open door.

"Isn't that something," Neil said. "I guess they have to come in so low to keep the cargo out of the trees."

"I'm afraid he may hang that DC-3 in the trees," Scott yelled back.

They opened one of the fire bundles and took out the equipment they would need to fight the imaginary fire.

Orange flagging marked the boundaries of the fire, and as Neil operated the chain saw, the rest of the Neds proceeded to dig a fire line around the flagging. This line was dug a foot wide and down to the clear soil. All the limbs and brush that extended over or near the line were also cleared away. These eager young fire fighters worked and sweated for two hours, stopping only long enough to take an occasional drink from the canteens that hung from their belts.

"These fires with no smoke and no heat aren't bad to work on," Scott told Neil.

"Yeah, this is the kind I'm going to order every time," Neil replied with a smile.

Once the imaginary fire was surrounded, the area around it was divided into sections. The Neds proceeded to comb over each section in search of small orange pieces of flagging. These represented sparks that the wind had supposedly carried out past the fire line.

Once the "fire" was out to Chuck and Ken's satisfaction, the Neds sat about retrieving and packing up the equipment and jump gear. Systematically, Scott stuffed the parachutes, jumpsuit, bedroll, and tools into the giant backpack. He forced it in by pushing with his feet.

"Don't forget the empty food cans," Neil reminded.

The canteens were tied on top where they could be reached easily.

Scott sat on a fallen log and removed his boots. He carefully smoothed the wrinkles from his two pair of socks. Then, like an athlete dressing for competition, he started with the toe laces and tightened his way up past the ankles and the eight inch top.

"A good pair of boots is a joy forever," Guy said as he watched Scott.

"Should be! These suckers are five times the price of a good pair of shoes," Scott answered.

"In this case you get what you pay for," Guy said sounding like a shoe salesman. "Have you ever been to the White Boot Company's factory in Spokane?"

"No, but I've seen their catalogue. I was surprised to see they call this boot the 'Smokejumper.'"

"Really?" Ralph asked, having overheard their conversation. "I'll bet you a beer that you just made that up."

"You're on, and Guy's my witness. I'll show you the catalogue when we get back to the barracks."

"I'll have to see it to believe it," Ralph persisted.

The packs weighed more than one hundred pounds. It was comical to see the Neds sit down in front of the packs, put their arms through the straps and then struggle to get on their feet.

"You see why smokejumpers are usually brought off fires by helicopters or by pack mules," Ken said, pointing to the monstrous backpacks. "But there will be times when packing will be the only way out."

"Remember to take care of your body. If something rubs, stop and fix it before you're crippled up," Chuck warned.

"OK, let's go," Ken said. "May the best man win!" Without a pack, Ken turned and headed down the trail for his afternoon stroll. Wobbling and weaving under their packs, the Neds followed. Scott's heavy pack felt terribly uncomfortable, straining every muscle and joint in his body. Then slowly his awkward gait found a more natural balance and rhythm. Scott worked to keep his mind off the strained muscles and straps that dug painfully into his shoulders. He refused to listen as his feet and legs begged for relief. Sweating profusely, step after step, he followed the pack in front of him; trance-like, Scott lost his perception of time and distance.

Rounding a bend in the trail, Scott saw that he was nearing the smokejumper base. He knew that no more than a half mile separated from camp and relief for his aching body. He was filled with pride and renewed strength now that he realized that he could complete the three-and-and-half mile packout without stopping.

Looking down the road, Scott could see four lumbering packs between him and the loft building. The two lead packs were bouncing up and down rapidly. Scott knew that the two leaders were jogging neck and neck down to the wire.

"Come on, Neil! Catch him, Big Fellow! Go! Hustle!" cheered the veteran smokejumpers who gathered at the finish. Everyone was excited as they congratulated Neil for being the first to cross the finish line.

Scott stumbled onto the lawn, and two of the 'old-timers' lifted the pack from his back.

"Pay up, pay the man who knows how to pick a winner," one of the guys said as he moved about collecting dollar bills. "I've always been good at selecting 'pack stock.' I knew Pretty Boy would take it hands down," He bragged, happily raking in his loot.

"Training is over!" Scott moaned as he dropped exhausted to the ground. The cool shade felt good to his sweat-soaked body.

"Congratulations! We didn't win, but we made it," Guy said.

"Congratulations!" Scott answered as he lay back with his eyes fixed on the brilliant blue sky.

Thirty minutes behind the others Ralph labored his pack across the finish. "Well, if it isn't Ned Bartlett," one of the veterans called out. "Where have you been? Did you stop for a nap?"

"Saving myself for the party tonight," Ralph answered struggling onto the lawn.

"Can you get me a date for tonight? I've heard you have lots of friends," the big money winner asked.

"No." Ralph answered flatly, seeing no humor in the harassment.

A party at North Beach is the traditional end of training. With a carnival spirit the Neds and Old-timers gathered with their friends to celebrate.

"What a place for a party!" Tex exclaimed, dragging his walking cast through the sand.

People visited as they milled between the snack table and ice-packed keg. Someone strummed a guitar and Guy joined in on his harmonica. The bright moonlight reflected off the water making visibility good; but, the colorful garb of the partiers was only seen in the circle of firelight that surrounded the giant bonfire.

"Circle up, I've got something for the Neds," Don Lent directed, stepping close to the fire.

"Ralph Myers," Don announced and Ralph walked out from the crowd. "Finally you're first, Ralph," Don said as the noisy crowd quieted momentarily. Don handed Ralph his smokejumper wings, then shook his hand. The wings were silver with a green fir tree in the center and a parachute canopy directly above it.

"All that work for this little pin," Ralph complained, his face shining with pride. Then he stepped back to show the pin to his attractive date. The rowdy crowd clapped and hooted.

"Scott Patrick!" Don announced the next name. Scott stepped out hesitantly accepting the pin, handshake, and broad smile. The crowd again cheered and clapped. Ducking back, Scott felt a sense of pride and accomplishment.

With the announcement of each Ned's name the party grew wilder. They stomped, cheered and yelled as they each received their wings.

"You are now qualified and certified," stated an 'old-timer,' "but you won't be bonafied until you've jumped on a real fire." A cheer of agreement rose into the night air.

"Time for the traditional Ned's skit," Tex, the Ned's wounded spokesman announced.

Wearing the hat Ken had worn during training, and eye-glasses made from the bottom of two Coke bottles held together with white tape, Tex tried to imitate Uncle Ken's voice. "Quit your complaining, you know you hired on to be tough!" Tex drawled in his southern accent as scenes from training were re-enacted in the firelight. The crowd loved the show and roared its approval.

When the skits were over, conversation, singing and laughter mingled and drifted in the cool night air.

Many of the old-timers insisted that this year's Neds were too aggressive and that they had forgotten their humble station in life. They mumbled, "What's this world coming to, anyway? These Neds are telling jump stories as if they were 'real' smokejumpers." One Ned was carried, thrashing and screaming, to the lake's edge and thrown in.

The night progressed and reasonable people went home, the others grew wilder. To the tune of The Battle Hymn of the Republic the male-dominated voices sang in uncoordinated harmony:

"There was blood upon the risers;
There was blood upon the chute,
There were intestines hanging
From his heavy logger boots.
Glory, glory what a hell
Of a way to die!
Glory, glory what a hell
Of a way to die."

Later still, things quieted down to softer singing and low conversation. Scott sat watching the fire, every star visible in the clear, mountain sky.

Scott wished he could share this experience with Julie. He felt a little lonely as he looked into the dying embers of the bonfire. Training, completed just today, seemed far behind him.

8

SMOKEJUMPER JUSTICE

Like a runner in the starting blocks, every muscle in Scott's body was primed. His eyes strained to follow the black dot as it splashed through the white water and flowed through the low ripples. About there! No, there! In a breath-taking flash Scott felt the hit. He jerked!

"I've got him! I got him this time," Scott hollered to Guy who stood fishing thirty yards away. The rush of the north fork of the Payette River drowned out his words, but he continued yelling excitedly. Twice before the trout had hit his gray hackle fly in that exact spot.

Scott's reflexes had been too slow to hook the shiny rainbow; but this time he had him. The trout leaped from the water with a violent shake, struggling to throw the hook from his mouth.

"What a fighter! He fought like a tiger," Scott said removing the hook from the thick, thirteen inch trout.

"I can't wait to show you some Cut-Throat trout from our high mountain lakes," Guy said. "We've got some big ones up there."

"I'm ready for them," Scott answered still impressed with the six trout they had caught. Their wet pants and tennis shoes sloshing with each step as they returned to camp.

SMOKEJUMPER

The rest of the weekend Scott spent much as the others were doing. He hung around the barracks, swam in the lake and laid on the beach. The sun's healing rays and the welcome sleep quickly restored him and the soreness left Scott's muscles. He caught up on his laundry and letter writing, and felt ready for what ever the fire season held in store.

Tex was hobbling around in his walking cast and a few other Neds nursed less serious injuries the Monday morning they gathered to draw for position on the jump roster.

Fifty-one men waited to draw for position on the jump list. The person drawing number one would be placed at the top and number fifty-one at the bottom. The men at the top of the roster would be the first to go on fires. When they returned to camp, their names would rotate to the bottom of the list.

Don Lent appeared on the deck. "We're ready to draw for position," he announced. Don held a hat over his head, as each smokejumper drew a slip of paper. Each man quickly looked at the slip he had drawn and reacted to what he saw written on it. One jumper shouted with delight, others groaned and looked disappointed.

Mouse, a small experienced jumper, grumbled, "About usual. Right in the middle, number twenty-six."

"All right! I'm in the first planeload," Scott yelled as he looked at the paper he held. "I'm number five."

"Not bad for a Ned," someone behind him remarked.

The men showed their numbers to Chuck, who wrote out the jump order on his clipboard. "B-z-z-z-z-z!" The buzzer on the loft building sounded one long blast. Everyone stopped and looked toward the sound.

"That's to show you new men what the buzzer sounds like," Don said. "When you hear that sound, stop and listen. The long blast lets you know we have a fire. The series of short blasts that will follow indicate the number of jumpers that will be going out."

"You'll have to be ready to go at any moment," Ken joined in. "There will be no excuse for not having the plane in the air within fifteen minutes."

Don began again, "The plane waits for no one and once you're in the air you may be gone from McCall for a few minutes or as long as a month."

Don and the others went back inside the office to determine work assignments now that the jump order was established. Excitement ran through the group as they realized a fire call could come at any moment.

"What number are you, Hardluck?" Mouse was asking Dave Gentry.

"Twenty-five. Not bad for usually having such bad luck," Dave answered.

"Oh, no! Not twenty-five! That can't be; I'm number twenty-six. I'm your J.P.!" Mouse moaned, then called to the group. "Can I swap numbers with anyone?"

"You'd better trade quick if you're going to, Mouse!" a voice from the crowd shouted. "No one will trade once they find out you're Hardluck's jump-partner."

Others joined in teasing Dave about his bad luck. Dave had received the "Golden Guideline" award at last summer's termination party. He had been chosen because he had the worst luck of anyone in the unit. The name "Hardluck" came with the award and it stuck like glue.

"You superstitious bunch of weirdos," Hardluck was yelling. "I'm no bad omen. I just had a couple of mishaps during training and missed a few of the good trips last summer, that's all."

But no one seemed to be buying Hardluck's proclamation of a turn-around in luck. Despite Mouse's best efforts, he remained Hardluck's J.P.

Chuck appeared on the deck with a list of work assignments and began assigning details. The first twenty smokejumpers were assigned to work projects close to the base. The next twenty would go on day-long jobs within driving distance of camp. The remaining jumpers would be sent to the backcountry where they would stay all week. The crews working away from camp would keep in touch by calling in on shortwave radios. The daily weather forecast would help the squad leaders determine how many men to keep near the base and how often those out of camp should call in.

Since Scott was at the top of the jump list, he was assigned to work in camp. His job would be painting the garage.

"Before you spread out to your work assignments, Jack needs to have a brief meeting with the Neds," Ken shouted from the platform.

"Over here," a big freckled-faced, redhead was calling. "Circle up, Neds! Circle up."

"What can this be about?" Scott asked Guy.

"Neds only. Doesn't sound good to me," Guy answered.

The nervous but not so naive group of first year jumpers gathered in a circle around the powerfully built redhead.

SMOKEJUMPER

"I'm Jack Wright," he said. He had a boyish look to his freckled face. His lower lip bulged with the tobacco that showed at the corner of his mouth. His gray T-shirt stating "Property of the Athletic Dept., University of Montana," met his faded Levis at a beltless waist. The Levis stopped short of his heavy boots.

"Seems we need to select the cowboy who will represent this outfit in the Council rodeo next week," Jack drawled as he turned slowly looking over each Ned. "Council is a little town thirty-five miles from here. It would break their hearts if the Smokejumpers weren't represented in their amateur rodeo," Jack added, swaggering with the power he held over the Neds.

"I'll bet it would break their hearts," Guy whispered under his breath.

"Dig into your pocket for a coin. Kneel on one knee and listen up while I tell you what's going to happen," Jack instructed. "This is called a 'Heads-Out,' a really neat procedure used for personnel selection. It's smokejumper tradition and it is used when we need to select someone or someones for a special purpose. It could be for a job everyone wants. Like today," Jack said with a sarcastic grin. "Or for a tough job nobody wants; maybe just to see who buys the pop or beer. It is very democratic because a coin plays no favorites and it has no conscience," Jack added with mocking seriousness.

"Neds only! It sounds real democratic," Guy grumbled unconvinced.

"Starting here with Neddy Ralph you will one at a time flip your coin in the air and let it land on the ground. If you flip a head, step back from the circle. You're eliminated! If you flip a tail, stay kneeling. You could be our C-O-W-B-O-Y!"

56

SMOKEJUMPER

Like sheep to the slaughter the Neds silently knelt with their coins ready. Jack spat a mouth full of tobacco juice in Ralph's direction saying, "OK, Ralphy Pear-butt, flip your coin."

Ralph's nervous thumb sent his four bit piece rotating high into the air. It landed at Jack's feet. "You're no cowboy, Ralphy," he motioned Ralph back from the circle.

"You sure it was a head? I couldn't see it," Neil said as he stood up.

"DOWN! Pretty Boy!" Jack commanded. "You don't have to see it. That's what I'm here for."

Neil moved quickly back to one knee.

"You're next Neddy Patrick" Jack pointed to Scott.

"I'm not going to flip. I wouldn't even know how to get on a horse," Scott stated flatly.

"Great, that's great," Jack said. "That means Scott is selected to ride in the bareback competition next week in Council. Contest over," Jack said calmly. "Smokejumper tradition has it that if you don't flip, you automatically lose. But you'll have to decide if you want to flip or not."

"Smokejumper justice," Scott muttered under his breath as he flipped his coin into the clear mountain air.

"A tail, Scott, you have a chance to be our representative and it would serve you right if you are," Jack hissed. "I don't like your negative attitude."

Only three Neds were left kneeling after the first round of flips. Scott was scared now. "What if I should lose?" Scott worried. "I couldn't possibly ride a bucking horse in a rodeo."

"That's it, a head," Jack said, motioning another jumper back from the circle leaving only Ned Suggins and Scott in the action.

Suggins' quarter rolled in the air landing face down. "A tail!" Scott screamed. "Now I just have to flip a head."

"No," Scout shouted. His coin bounced to a stop tail up.

Suggins flipped again, "B-E-A-U-T-I-F-U-L!" George Washington's shiny face smiled up from his quarter.

"I can still match you," Scott said watching his coin dance above the ground, as if in slow motion.

"A head! a head! a head!" Scott pleaded as the coin rolled to a stop. It was tails!

"Comin' out of Chute Number Five, it's C-O-W-B-O-Y Patrick," Jack announced, delight in his voice.

After cheering the winner, the Neds headed in varying directions to their assigned work details.

"I just won't do it," Scott muttered. "You can't make me. It is not part of my job."

"I'm sure you will once you get used to the idea," Jack said. "You just have to start thinking of yourself as a cowboy." Jack started walking to the tool shed to get out the painting supplies.

"That's a bunch of crap if I've ever heard it," Scott grumbled to himself as he followed Jack.

"A real glamorous job, this smokejumping," Guy said sarcastically, as he dipped his brush into the light green paint.

"Yeah," Jack responded. "We get some boring jobs all right, but there is an element of excitement to this job you don't find in most. We live with the expectation that at any moment we could get a fire call. We could get a call to go most anywhere, to that mountain over there," Jack said pointing, "Or we could go to Alaska. Then again, we could be painting most all summer. It's that unknown factor that keeps you going," he added emphasizing his point by spitting some brown juice on the ground.

"I wish we would get called to Alaska," Scott said. "I hope we get called someplace. I can't ride in that rodeo!"

"Well, did you ever think you could jump out of an airplane?" Guy asked trying to help.

"That's different!" Scott said, "I've had a month of training for that. I could get killed by a bucking horse. I've only been on horses a couple of times in my life."

"Well, my first plane ride I parachuted out," Guy said, "I've taken off in an airplane seven times and I haven't landed yet."

"Those landings are scary," Jack said laughing.

"I'm too young to get killed in a rodeo," Scott continued to complain.

"You don't think you can get killed jumping out of an airplane?" Jack questioned. "We have a Ned ride at Council every year, and we haven't lost anyone yet."

"Y-E-T!" Scott said.

"We've had a few broken bones, but nothing serious," Jack gave the historic perspective.

"Just a few broken bones," Scott parroted. "Now I feel better. You sure know how to shape up a guy's confidence."

"I'm through talking about that rodeo," Jack said. "If you stop thinking about it, you won't be so nerved up and edgy."

"I just won't do it," Scott said quietly to himself, with doubt in his voice.

After a day of painting Scott and Guy returned to the

59

barracks.

"Who put all this stuff on my bunk?" Scott asked, holding up a pair of well worn leather chaps. A metallic ring sounded as a pair of spurs fell to the floor.

"The cowboy boots look like a pair I saw Tex wearing," Guy answered. "Don't worry! People will be back to claim their stuff after the rodeo."

"Who's going to a rodeo? I don't have to you know," Scott added. "This whole joke has gotten out of hand."

"Looks like a cowboy hat is all you need," Ralph said walking toward the shower room with a towel over his shoulder.

Scott pushed the western gear onto the floor and laid out on his bunk.

Morning calisthenics had loosened Scott's muscles. He felt good as he moved toward the tool shed to get out the paint brushes.

"Beautiful weather for a cowboy contest," Tony said in a teasing voice as his mustache raised revealing a broad smile. Tony had black hair and a twinkle in his brown eyes. He was a native Idahoan with family roots in Basque Spain.

"Just two more days and you won't have to worry about this. It'll all be over," Guy said, having overheard the conversation.

"I'm not worried. I'm not doing it." Scott muttered under his breath, so the others wouldn't hear and get on his case.

Ken stepped into the tool shed behind Scott and began selecting tools.

"I'm worried, Ken. They can't make me ride in that stupid

rodeo, can they?" Scott asked after seeing they were alone.

"Nobody can make you do anything," Ken said reassuringly. Then he added, "But I reckon you'll want to."

"It would be suicide! Nobody has the right to ask that of anyone," Scott pleaded.

"No one has ever gotten killed at the Council rodeo," Ken said, looking surprised at Scott's fear. "A broken bone or two, maybe."

"B-Z-Z-Z-Z-Z!" The long blast of the buzzer shattered the cool morning air. Scott froze in his tracks. It was followed by ten short, evenly spaced blasts. His heart raced! He was reprieved! There was justice in the world after all.

9

FIRE CALL

"Is it the real thing?" Scott asked in disbelief.

"Of course," Ken answered.

The pilot had the propellers turning when they reached the airport. Dust and dirt blew in Scott's face as he lumbered onto the plane. The ten heavily clad men sat packed in among the fire gear as the graceful blue and white Twin Otter lifted them into the sky. It was built to meet the demands of wilderness flying, with special built jet-prop twin engines suitable for the short backcountry landing fields.

Wayne Garrison put his hand on Scott's shoulder to steady himself while he wrote the parachute numbers on his spotter's report.

"Where's the fire?" Scott asked as Wayne checked his equipment.

"Hey, cowboy! It's you," Wayne said. "Fire is on the west side near Hell's Canyon. Look! We're flying over Council now," Wayne pointed.

"The rodeo is tomorrow. I probably won't be off this fire in time to go," Scott said looking down on the small town.

"Well, we will get you back if we can," Wayne added patting Scott on the back.

"Don't try too hard," Scott said, then thought to himself, "I can't seem to convince people that I can't ride a horse. Here I am on my way to parachute out over a forest fire, and I'm worried about a stupid rodeo."

"The plane wasn't thirty minutes west of McCall when Scott saw the big cloud of whitish smoke.

"You'll get a lot of help on this one; it's by the road," Wayne said. "West of McCall is good jump country," he continued. "It has grassy slopes at the lower elevations and scattered timber with open ridges higher up."

Off to the right of the plane Scott caught a glimpse of the beautiful Seven Devils Mountains in the morning sun. They lay just east of the famed Hell's Canyon, the deepest canyon in all of North America.

Wayne held his hand on the cable that ran the length of the plane as he moved back toward the tail section. Stopping, he told the crew, "The dispatch says a gas truck tipped over and started this fire. The wreck ignited the gas and it spilled into Brownlee Creek. The stream spread the fire down both banks for about half a mile. It hasn't reached the timber yet," Wayne continued, "but it's burning a lot of grass."

"Is that why the smoke's so light colored?" Scott asked.

"Yes," Wayne answered, as he moved closer to the open door.

The plane began flying a circular pattern over the grass fire. The smell of the burning grass was strong in the airplane.

Leaning toward Neil, Scott said, "I thought you were going to order fires without smoke."

With a nervous laugh Neil responded, "Yeah, my order must have gotten screwed up someplace."

SMOKEJUMPER

Scott realized that Neil was excited too, as he nervously adjusted his equipment. All ten jumpers watched Wayne drop the wind streamers and study them carefully as they glided toward the ground. Jack leaned against the side of the plane with his eyes closed, recovering from last night's party.

In sets of two, the jumpers took their places in the open door. Wayne held his head close to their helmets to give them the information they would need to safely land at the edge of the fire.

Neil was the first jumper of the two-man stick that would precede Jack and Scott. As they got their instructions, Scott pulled his face mask down, tightened his leg straps, and pulled on his gloves, preparing himself for the jump. Neil and his jump partner balanced in the open door, one behind the other. The wind pulled at Neil's collar and hair as he leaned his head out the open door. The levelness of the plane and the sound of the twin engines being cut back indicated the drop zone was approaching. Neil religiously crossed himself just as Wayne slapped the back of his leg, and both jumpers bailed out into the open air.

Now it was Scott's turn. He hooked his static-line to the cable that ran the length of the plane. "The only wind is high! Face the plane once your chute opens, and when you get a feel for the drift, work your way in," Wayne's calm voice spoke into the ear hole of Scott's helmet.

"Give me some room." Scott told Jack as he remembered tangling chutes with Tex.

"Don't give me orders, NED!" Jack answered in a cranky voice that smelled of stale tobacco and last night's beer.

The open door, the noise, the rushing air, and then the dry

sting of smoke contributed to Scott's confusion and fear as they approached the drop zone. His heart pounded, but he remained in control as he looked through the thin layer of smoke that hung above the dry grassy mountains of the Hell's Canyon area.

"Go!" Wayne yelled. Scott felt the slap on his leg and he knew Jack would be running up his back if he hesitated a moment.

"P-a-t-r-i-c-k," Scott heard himself howl as he tumbled from the plane, concentrating on keeping his eyes wide open. He not only kept his eyes open; he glued them on the horizon. The drummed-in-lessons from Ned training seemed to have become automatic.

Just as Scott was running out of breath, the magnificent tug of his parachute taking air swung him beneath the brightly colored canopy.

"Beautiful!" Scott said out loud as he visually checked the swollen nylon above his head. "I'm doing fine," he added as he glimpsed Jack's chute over his shoulder.

"The old-timers were right. Wayne reads the drift perfectly," Scott thought to himself, as he found the air to be just as Wayne had said. Looking down from where he swung beneath the thirty-two-foot parachute, Scott could see that the rolling, grassy hills below would make an inviting landing spot.

The cargo for Scott's planeload had little more than reached the ground when the DC-3 appeared and began dropping jumpers on the next ridge. Four planeloads of jumpers had been "rained" down around the fire in less than two hours.

The bright sun hadn't yet heated the canyon air, and there was no wind as Scott chopped and dug at the grass and wild

The magnificent tug of Scott's parachute taking air swung him beneath the brightly colored canopy.

daisies that covered the mountain. The crew moved at a walk cutting a ditch six inches deep and a foot wide in the sandy soil. The trail was anchored to out-croppings of rock on the ridges and the brush-filled draws slowed the jumpers to a crawl as they snaked a course along the fire's edge.

"This could turn into work," Guy said as he straightened up and mopped his forehead with his shirtsleeve.

"Sure could," Scott agreed. "I can feel the blisters already."

"This one is gravy!" Jack said. "You Neds wait until you get on a fire that burns trees, not just grass. Look! There are trucks unloading ground pounders now," Jack pointed to the road with his freckled hand. "We've got enough men on this little grass fire to douse it if we all spit."

The ground crews began building lines up from the bottom as the jumpers sealed off the top and started working down the flanks of the fire. By 1500 hours the three-hundred-acre grass fire was under control. Once the fire had been stopped, it cooled quickly.

"If it had reached the timber one hundred yards up the mountain, it would have been a different story," Scott thought.

"It's not often you can jump a fire in the morning and sleep in the barracks that very night," Jack said.

"I'm getting worried again," Scott said to Guy.

"Nothing to worry about, this baby isn't going anywhere," Guy answered with a look of confusion on his face.

"That's what's got me worried. If we get back to McCall by tomorrow morning I'll be a cowboy in that wild west show in Council," Scott said.

"Oh," Guy said as if he hadn't heard a word.

SMOKEJUMPER

"Let's have some food and pack our stuff to the road," Jack said. "Ken is with a crew on the next ridge. I talked with him on the radio and he said a bus would pick us up at 1700 hours."

As Scott pawed through the food bag, Jack directed, "Hand me a can of John Wayne crackers to go with this salmon." Then fumbling in his pocket he drew out a compact can opener an inch long and a half inch wide. "That's one thing the government did right. I can hardly believe the army developed this efficient little honey," he said pulling the blade open. "This has got to be one of the great inventions of the world," Jack raved on as he worked the top off his can of salmon.

"The ole P-38 is one of the handiest things I know for an outdoorsman," Scott agreed. "We should be saving these out of every ration pack, someday I think they could be valuable."

"We could sell them to folks touring the loft for a quarter apiece," Neil said as he hunkered over his can of fruit. "That way we could make some money for the athletic fund."

"Oh Good! Then I suppose we could pay the entry fee for more Neds to ride in the Council rodeo," Scott said with tension in his stomach.

Looking west, Scott could see across the canyon to the beau--tiful Wallowa-Whitman Forest of Oregon, but the steepness of the canyon blocked his view of the Snake River below. "What a view," he said, handing Jack the crackers.Then turning to the north he saw the timbered mountains rising majestically into the skyline.

After lunch Scott gathered all his fire-fighting gear and supplies into a pile. Then he collected his jumpsuit and both parachutes. "Here we go again," he thought to himself, as he wrestled his gear into the packsack.

"Make your pack tight so it won't fly apart if it gets rough treatment. Keep out your let-down rope," Jack said. "I'll show you something you didn't learn in Neddy school; it'll save you a lot of time and work."

The road was close, no more than a mile below them. "Straight below!" Scott thought as he peered down.

Helping each other up, the jumpers moved cautiously about a hundred yards to where a cliff blocked their progress. From the edge of the cliff, getting to the road below seemed impossible. "This country's steeper than the back of God's head," Neil said in discouragement.

"Relax, Neil, while I show you Neds a trick or two," Jack said. "Now put down your packs and watch carefully." Jack tied his let-down rope to his pack, and held on to the rope as he gave the pack a roll down the steep cliff. He fed the line out a few feet at a time, until the bundle had bounced nearly a hundred feet, then he crept down to it, easing himself along slowly. "Now that's how the experts do it," Jack said. "But don't let it get away from you or you'll be forever trying to rescue your smashed equipment from the canyon."

They all proceeded in a similar manner, letting out the rope and edging down to it. The ropes got caught on bushes and rocks, and it required continuous attention to keep the bundles moving. At times, the heavy weight of the pack seemed more in control of the situation than the jumper who was holding the other end of the rope.

The last quarter of a mile to the road was a more reasonable slope, and Scott and the others carried their packs in the traditional manner. When they reached the creek, they were glad to soak their hot, tired feet and splash cool water over their bodies before loading into the bus.

"Our cowboy is going to make the BIG RODEO after all," Jack announced to the cheering busload of jumpers. Jack's hair and face were filthy from fire fighting and tobacco tracks ran down his chin.

"Did I tell you that the athletic fund pays your entry fee, Ned?" Jack questioned.

"About three times," Scott said under his breath. "I'm so glad you keep reminind me; I would hate to be paying for the opportunity of getting killed. It won't cost me a dime, just my life," Scott moaned with sarcastic resignation in his voice.

"How many times do I have to tell you? No one has ever been killed at the Council rodeo," Jack said in disgust.

"I feel better now. A broken bone is probably all I can count on," Scott said. "Unless, of course, I set a record by being the first fatality."

In their usual spirit of poor taste, the old-timers began to tease and harass the first-year men. After a while, Ken, with a bearing of authority, announced, "Enough is Enough! These Neds just jumped their first fire, which makes them qualified, certified, and bonafide smokejumpers!"

The old-timers booed, then they settled back and relaxed.

It was dark when the bus rolled into the smokejumper camp. Half awake, Scott thought only of a hot shower and his bunk, but Ken's voice reminded him of duty, "Let's get this gear cleaned up and repacked so we'll be ready for the next fire."

Scott found his name on the new jump roster. "I'm number

thirteen," he said. "I hope that isn't unlucky."

"The list doesn't change much when nearly everyone goes on the same fire," Ken said. "They move us squad leaders around on the jump list to keep us spaced out. I've been moved to number fourteen, so it looks like you and I are J.P.'s," Ken added.

"Great!" Scott said.

"Your old J.P. is still going to the rodeo with you tomorrow," Jack interrupted. His voice was filled with excitement.

"As tired as I am I would rather go on another fire than to that rodeo," Scott thought. But there was no more talk as they finished the remaining chores and headed up the hill.

"Qualified, certified, and bonafide smokejumpers," Ken's words ran through Scott's mind as he went to sleep.

10

COWBOY SCOTT

"Well you look like a cowboy," Guy said.

"I hope I can fool that horse," Scott answered, placing the cowboy hat on his head. "Just like these boots, the hat doesn't fit either."

"Some people would bitch if they were hung with a new rope," Guy protested. "Where did you get that hat anyway?"

"When I got back from the fire I found it and this on my bed," Scott said, holding a large book with a brown home-made wrapper up for Guy's inspection.

"Cowboy's Training Manual," Guy read the crudely written label.

"Look at this," Scott said, opening the book. Someone had cut the center out of the pages and inserted a pint of Jim Beam whiskey.

"Consume this thirty minutes before your ride, lean back and stay loose," Scott read the note attached to the bottle.

"See! Everyone wants to help our rodeo hero," Guy said with a laugh.

Scott and Jack were loading into Jack's beat-up Ford for the thirty-five mile ride to Council when Ken walked up.

"Sorry more of us can't go down and cheer you on, but the weatherman says we're to get lightning. Good luck anyway,"

Ken said.

"Thanks," Scott answered politely. Then under his breath, "I'm going to need it."

The Ford pulled onto the highway. Jack was wearing Levis, cowboy boots and a western shirt with a small floral pattern. "We'll be too late for the barbecue and parade; but we'll have time for a few beers before the rodeo and of course there is always the dance later," Jack was excited as he spoke. "You're awfully quiet, Ned, are you still worried?"

"Don't tell me again. I know that no one has ever been killed in the Council rodeo," Scott answered in a sarcastic voice. "I'm not worried about that or anything else. I just don't want to talk. Anything wrong with that?" Scott snapped as he yawned and stretched.

"You'll soon be sitting on a bucking horse and you're bored?" Jack asked.

"I'm not bored, I'm scared. I yawn when I'm scared. OK with you?" Scott snapped again.

"We had better get started on that pint of Jim Beam, you're tight as a drum," Jack said.

"No, thanks! The state I'm in it would just make me sick," Scott said, his voice softer now.

"Hand 'old Jim' over here," Jack said, "I'll show you what it's for."

"Pull over for a minute Jack," Scott said. Jack stopped the old Ford and Scott got out and walked to the driver's side. "Bump over, I'll drive you and Mr. Jim Beam to Council," Scott said getting behind the wheel.

Between long drinks from the whiskey bottle Jack spat tobacco juice into the can he kept in front of his seat. Jack was having a great time singing along with the western music provided by KMCL McCall, on the car radio. He generously offered Scott the bottle, but didn't object when Scott passed it back without participating.

The rodeo grounds were decked out in flags and banners as the battered blue Ford glided past. Main street was decorated too. Scott reined "Big Blue" to a stop directly in front of a saloon.

"Put on those chaps and spurs. People will buy us free drinks if they can see you're a contestant," Jack directed, dropping the empty whiskey bottle to the floor.

"I'll put them on when I'm ready to ride," Scott's annoyance came through clearly. "If you're interested in free drinks, put that stuff on yourself and I'll even let you ride for me." Scott piled out and started into a crowded bar. Jack swayed behind him.

"I'll take a beer," Scott said after Jack had placed his order with the bartender. The place was noisy and smoke filled.

B-R-O-O-M, B-R-O-O-O-M, B-R-O-O-O-M came the sound of someone revving a motorcycle in the street. "What is that?" Jack muttered.

"It's either a motorcycle or a DC-3 doing a pre-take-off check-out," Scott yelled above the roar.

B-R-O-O-M, B-R-O-O-O-M, B-R-O-O-O-M the noise continued. "That guy is proud of that thing" Jack complained.

The noise stopped and moments later three figures came through the door. The noisy crowd quieted momentarily letting the intruders know that their disturbance was not appreciated.

74

SMOKEJUMPER

The smaller man and the woman moved chairs up to a crowded table directly behind where Jack and Scott stood at the bar. Their barrel shaped companion stepped to the bar. He appeared to be about thirty. His face was framed with a full beard and topped with a yachting cap. His gold earring caught Scott's eye, but he tried not to stare. The cyclist stood next to Scott. His hairy body protruded from a sleeveless Levi jacket. BROTHER WHEELS was written in the shape of a circle on his back, and inside the circle was a picture of the Road Runner.

"B-r-o-o-m, b-r-o-o-m, b-r-o-o-o-m," Jack said under his breath. Low at first and then increasing in volume.

"What are you doing," Scott asked in a whisper not wanting the giant at his elbow to hear.

"Nothing," Jack said laughing.

"B-R-O-O-M, B-R-O-O-M," Jack started up louder this time.

"You're crazy," Scott warned.

The bar went silent and the giant stained form stepped behind Scott and put his hand on Jack's shoulder.

"You don't mean anything by that do you?" the deep voice asked.

"No, just having some fun," Jack answered respectfully. "I don't want any trouble. Let's forget it." Jack extended his hand for a shake.

"Good," said the stranger as he accepted Jack's hand. "I don't think you could give me much trouble anyway."

The defensive noseguard for the University of Montana seemed docile as a puppy as he shook the big hand.

Then "B-R-O-O-M, B-R-O-O-M," sounded loud and clear

from Jack's mouth again, as he gripped the giant hand and twisted to the right as if it were a motorcycle throttle.

"JACK!" Scott shouted as he tried to warn him of the left fist headed for his face. Scott clasped his hands together as he spun around planting his right elbow deep into the hairy chest.

"Clear out," Jack yelled, tackling into the cyclist and both bodies dropped squarely across the table behind them. Glasses and bottles emptied their contents into the air and with a crash, furniture flew in pieces. The younger 'Brother Wheels' started for Scott as his female companion kicked at Jack's exposed ribs, with her moccasined feet. Scott moved quickly to escape the oncoming rush and the oversized cowboy hat fell over his eyes, and he couldn't see what hit him.

Noise and confusion reigned, as people tried to move out of the path of the brawl. Then as suddenly as it had all started, the place went deathly silent. Scott pushed his hat back so he could see, but someone had turned on the lights and they temporarily blinded him.

"You don't fight in here," said a stern voice from the bar. The barrel on the pistol he held looked like a short piece of stove pipe from where Scott sat in the middle of the floor.

"These folks won't cause you any more trouble," announced the Adam's County sheriff from where he appeared in the open doorway.

Scott felt his heart sink to his stomach as the sheriff ordered them to his waiting car.

11

A ROUGH RIDE AND A

BLEEPING LESSON

Routinely the jumpers grouped behind the loft to start their day. Don stepped out on the deck. "I heard there was some trouble in Council yesterday. I don't want any details or I may have to fire someone. Doggone it! I live in this community. You guys raise cane all summer, then leave. It isn't fair, so listen to this! I'm only going to say it once, and you had better understand it. You start something and get put in jail, I'll leave you there to rot, and should you get out, you won't have a job," Don threatened, the veins in his neck protruding with anger.

The jumpers listened quietly as they looked at the ground. Don's face relaxed. "I realize that some of the loggers and ranchers around this country like nothing better than adding a smokejumper's scalp to their belt, but it takes two to make a fight. You'll just have to learn to walk away from trouble. Maybe even stay out of those places. Just don't expect me to go out on a limb for you. That's all I'm going to say on the subject," Don finished and darted back into the loft.

"Send you down to represent us in the rodeo and you end up in jail. Some representative!" Tony said as they moved to the training field for morning calisthenics. "You didn't even make it to the rodeo."

"We weren't put in jail," Scott said sheepishly. "We were just held at the jail until damages were paid."

"Big difference, Jailbird," a veteran standing by chipped in.

"Scott Jailbird! You sure were right. You are no cowboy," someone else added as exercises started.

Scott gave up trying to clarify his story.

Following morning calisthenics the group split up for work details. Scott's crew worked close to camp, repairing fences for a few days.

"Tony, didn't I tell you there would be lots of women in town last weekend?" Ralph said.

"You sure did, but you forgot to say they would all have a boyfriend with them," Tony answered.

"You're hopeless, I think I'll give up on you and Patrick," Ralph complained. "But then I forgot Patrick's a fighter, not a lover."

"Forget it," Scott said. "I'm neither one."

After several days of fence mending a thunder storm crossed central Idaho. When Scott's detail returned to camp they were met by Don Lent. "A planeload of jumpers were dropped east of here and two planeloads will be held on standby until dark," Don explained.

"You mean we get paid for just waiting around?" Ralph questioned.

"If there is work that needs to be done, you do it; if there isn't, you just need to be available," Ken said.

"Man, that's all right!" Ralph exclaimed. "That's the best

thing I've heard of."

After dinner a volleyball game was organized.

"You guys have to take Hardluck," an old timer said. "We don't want to lose."

"No! You get him!" responded Jack. "We had him last time." Then Jack thought for a moment and said, "We'll take Hardluck if you'll take Bartlett Pear-butt." That settled the teams but the harassment and horseplay continued. Hardluck and Ralph were first, but no one was left out, not even Jailbird Patrick.

The game got underway and in the heat of the battle all else was forgotten. Heavy boots pounded dust from the already hard-packed court. Scott's team faced certain defeat when they were saved by the buzzer, blasting out a call for sixteen smoke-jumpers.

The clowning smokejumpers ran from the volleyball court as they began their transformation into a smoothly functioning fire-fighting team. Excitement rushed through Scott's body.

Within minutes the top sixteen men on the jump list were in the DC-3 flying over Jughandle Mountain.

"What a contrast this country is to the area west of McCall," Scott thought. "The west side is much gentler, with rolling ridge tops and logging roads scattered through the timbered slopes."

The plane flew east over the first ridges and Scott knew he was in love, in love with the beautiful country that stretched below. The sun lit up the granite cliffs and there were no signs of civilization. After an hour of flying, Scott placed his head back and rested it on his parachute. The hardware of the harness dug into his back, and the suit was hot and uncomfortable.

SMOKEJUMPER

They continued over more than a million acres of the forest known as the Idaho Primitive Area. In every direction Scott could see hundreds of timbered mountains stretching about him.

Don Lent sat in the co-pilot's seat and Ken was crunched in a corner of the plane with his eyes closed and his head bobbing to one side. The others seemed lost in their private thoughts. Without warning, the plane banked sharply and dropped down into a canyon. Startled, Ken jerked awake, "Are we there?" he asked.

"I don't know," Scott said, pressing his face against the window, searching for smoke. They made several passes down the same ridge, and each time they hit the rough air spilling over it. The plane jerked and bounced. Scott leaned back against the fuselage and closed his eyes as his stomach rolled and a bitter taste rose in his throat.

The plane climbed and banked, and the forces of gravity tugged relentlessly at Scott's body. He was fighting to ignore the saliva that was building up in his mouth. Jack handed him a plastic bag.

"Looks like Mrs. Patrick's little boy, Scotty, may need a barf bag," Jack said. Scott took the bag without smiling. He felt terrible.

Guy was sick too. He moved to the open door of the plane, hung his head out in the wind and vomited. Vomit rained into the plane, driven by the prop-blast that whirled through the open door. Everyone inside was speckled with the brown-colored vomit. Scott's body shuddered at the sight and smell as he held the bag to his face. Typically, this group would have had a lot to say to Guy, but no one had the strength right now.

80

SMOKEJUMPER

The jumpers were too sick to care when Don's voice announced, "There's the fire!" Being the spotter, Don put on his emergency parachute and moved to the open door in the tail section.

Scott felt the plane moving in a familiar circle and knew Don was dropping the crepe paper streamers to check the wind direction. He forced himself to open his eyes and look for his helmet. He could see Don speak into the microphone as he directed the pilot over the jump spot. Then Don threw the streamers and started the stopwatch he held in his left hand. Scott prayed that he wouldn't need the barf bag again once he got his helmet on and the face mask pulled into place.

"Two men," Ken said, interpreting Don's signal of two fingers raised in the air.

"Oh good! I'm number three," Scott thought with relief, as he removed his helmet and leaned back.

Guy and Jack were to jump together in a two-man stick. Guy looked pale as he leaned into the open doorway and awaited the signal to jump. The slap on his leg came and both figures were swallowed up by the turbulence outside the open door. With a noticeable increase in wind noise and the sound of the engines accelerating, they were gone.

The plane circled the jump spot one more time; then it dove down the ridge making the cargo run. Scott's heart seemed to stop as the sound of the engines grew quiet, and the plane glided lower and lower. Don knelt beside the cargo, his arms straining to keep it from being sucked out the door. They continued to lose altitude.

Scott braced himself. "I'm looking straight out at the trees on the ridge," he told himself nervously.

The treetops seemed to almost brush the vibrating wings. "D-i-n-g-g!" Scott jerked in fear. "What was wrong?"

Don responded by giving the pack a push. The cargo cleared the doorway, falling free of the plane. At that moment, the engines roared and Scott felt a surge of strength move through the old DC-3 as it began to climb back into the safety of the sky.

"Cargo away," Don yelled into the mike.

The plane gained a safe altitude and began to circle the jump spot to check on the men and the cargo. As Don looked for the large letter "L" on the ground that signified all were safe, Scott saw that Guy was hanging near the top of a tree.

"Poor devil," Scott said to himself, wondering what it would be like to try to get out of a tree that size if you were sick. Scott had forgotten his own sickness in the excitement of the cargo drop, but again he was thankful that this fire wasn't his.

It was dusk as the plane headed back toward McCall. Scott was no longer airsick, but he wasn't feeling good. He was glad to be going home, looking forward to a hot shower, dinner, and a good night's sleep.

Then the plane banked into a sharp turn. "What's going on?" Scott asked.

"We've found another fire," Ken said, reaching for his helmet.

Don moved to the open door and removed the safety strap. Still hoping it wasn't so, Scott moved into position as number one jumper, snapping down his face mask as he went. Ken, in the number two position, also readied himself for the jump. Don pointed out a slight trail of smoke rising out of a lush carpet of green timber. "I'll let you out right over the smoke. Pick a small tree," Don yelled over the roar of the open door. "There is no opening in the trees big enough for a jump spot, but there is no wind to worry about either."

Scott leaned forward and the prop-blast rattled through the ear hole in his helmet. He marvelled at Don's ability to keep the location of the fire straight. The low timbered ridges all looked alike to him.

As the plane approached the drop zone, adrenalin shot through Scott's body. He felt the slap of Don's hand on the calf of his leg, and his reflexes carried him out the open door. Scott held his breath but kept his eyes open. Then he felt the shock of being hauled up short, and he knew his parachute had opened.

"But what had happened?" Scott suddenly knew something was wrong, and terror shot through him. The chute was holding him in an upright position, but he couldn't get his head back to check it. His body twisted helplessly in the air! "My lines are twisted!" Scott's mind raced frantically.

"What do I do?" he asked himself, as he continued to spin. Scott remembered that he first needed to determine the rate of his descent by locating his jump partner. He held his right hand tight to the silver ripcord of his reserve chute in case he should need it.

"There's Ken!" Scott was relieved to see that both chutes were falling at the same speed. He loosened his grip on the ripcord. "I'm twisted, but my canopy is open. I won't have to pull my reserve," he thought.

For what seemed an eternity, Scott continued to spin, unwinding and drifting at the whim of the air currents as he floated above the timber. Finally, with one last jerk, he was free. His relief, however, was short-lived as he realized he was lost and didn't know where the fire was. "I could end up a mile from Ken with no idea of which way to go in the darkness," Scott thought, as his eyes frantically scanned the ground below. He pulled on his right guideline and made a searching half turn. Catching a glimpse of Ken's chute as it disappeared into the trees, he turned and headed toward it, hoping to make up for lost ground. But the trees came quickly up at him now and he crashed into their tops.

Scott grabbed for a limb, but missed it. His second attempt left him swinging with both arms over a branch; his feet moving wildly, but he couldn't find a second source of support. Scott was breathing deeply from the strain of holding on, and he could hardly see in the growing darkness. The limb to which he was clinging made a loud cracking sound, and suddenly he was falling again. Scott felt as if he were falling in slow motion. He hit the ground on his right side and rolled three times before he came to a stop, shaken and out of wind.

"Are you OK?" Scott heard a voice calling. He didn't feel like moving or answering, but as the air began to pour back into his lungs, he moved in an attempt to see how badly he was hurt. His arms seemed to work, and his legs, too! Scott couldn't believe it! He apparently wasn't injured at all!

"I'm OK!" he yelled back in an amazed voice.

By the time he had packed up his parachutes and jumpsuit, and strapped them to his back, the airplane had gone and it was dark.

"H-o-o-t," Scott called out as loudly as he could, hoping for a response from Ken. He wasn't sure from what direction Ken's inquiry had come. He waited a couple of minutes in the oppressive dark silence, then he gave out another loud, long, "H-o-o-t."

This time he heard a clear "H-o-o-t" in reply. It came from his right and with relief Scott moved toward it. Every thirty or forty yards he would stop and hoot, and Ken would send back a reassuring answer. In a few minutes Scott was close enough to hear Ken chopping on a log. When Scott approached him, he saw Ken was working by the light of his flashlight.

"Thanks for the help, Cowboy," Ken said with a smile as Scott walked up. He had the small fire all lined and almost out. "We'll have to fall a snag or two tomorrow when it's light," he added, "But now let's make a camp and eat."

Scott looked up at the old snag that reached into the air for a hundred and twenty feet, and knew that their work would be cut out for them in the morning. The three-and-a-half-foot trunk would give Scott more practice with the crosscut saw than he had ever had in his life. The misery whip, as the saw is called, lay near the fire packs.

"I could see from the plane that this big snag had been hit by lightning," Ken said. Hunks of freshly splintered wood were lying about. Ken showed Scott how the lightning had broken out the top of the snag and ripped out bark and wood on its spiraling path to the ground. High up near the top were glowing coals indicating that the heat from the strike had ignited a pitchy "catface."

"I thought about asking Don to drop us a chain saw instead of this misery whip," Ken continued, "But I figured we would be

85

doing some packing to get out of here, and I didn't want the added weight of the saw and gas. By the way, what took you so long to get to the fire, Ned? I went ahead and put out the double L's after you said you were all right, or that airplane would have run out of gas circling and waiting for you," Ken said.

Scott sheepishly began to tell Ken of his adventures. "I was twisted up and then I thought I was going to be killed when I fell out of the tree I hit. I'm just thankful that it was only a small lodgepole and not one of those monstrous yellow pines."

"Good eye for a Ned," Ken laughed. "Your eyes were so big when you left the plane, I wasn't sure if you would be able to tell a big tree from a little one."

Scott didn't bother to tell Ken that he had hit the smaller tree simply by chance. Scott felt comfortable talking with Ken, and proceeded to tell him in detail about his harrowing jump. Ken listened in a concerned manner, which encouraged Scott to tell the whole story.

"Ya' done good, Neddy Patrick, and you might have had some luck," Ken declared when Scott had finished. Then he directed, "You build a cooking fire and I'll stretch a cargo chute up between a couple of trees to make a tent, just in case it should rain."

Once the campfire was going, Ken picked out a can of chili beans and dropped them into it.

"That'll blow up, won't it?" Scott asked.

"Not if you're a good bleeper," Ken said, then warned, "Don't try this unless you're ready to pay close attention to what you're doing." As Ken watched the can closely in the firelight, he recalled, "Your jump today reminds me of a time I was jumping in New Mexico and I nearly hung up on a big yellow pine. I drifted in close to this two-hundred-foot tree and hit into it. Not wanting to hang up on a big limb I saw in my path, and knowing I couldn't miss it, I decided to kick hard with my feet and break it off so my parachute wouldn't catch on it. I was coiled like a spring and when my boots touched the limb, I straightened out with all my weight and strength. But to my surprise, the limb held and my body jolted to a stop. I sat there like a big eagle on this limb," Ken paused, smiling reflectively, and Scott wondered if he would ever go on with his story.

"Bleep," came the sound from the chili can, one end bulging out.

"That's one. Get ready," Ken said.

"Bleep," it sounded again, and like a cat, Ken flipped the can out of the fire with his shovel.

"Now the chili's heated through and just right for a feast," Ken bragged as he began opening the can with his P-38 opener. He explained to Scott the secret of opening a hot bleeped can without losing all its contents as a result of the built-up pressure.

"OK, OK, my bleeping lesson is complete," Scott said impatiently. "How did you get off that limb?"

"Oh, you were listening!" Ken laughed and then continued. "Well, I was hunkered on the limb, kind of dazed, and my parachute fell in front of me and kept goin'. I knew I was in trouble if I didn't act fast. In a flash I knew what I had to do. Like a bird, I jumped out into the air again and began to fall. Falling faster than the fluttering parachute, I got below it and felt it inflate again. It caught my weight just twenty or thirty feet above the ground, so I'm still around bleeping food," he chuckled and then got more serious again. "I hope I didn't make the bleeping look too easy. A five-second delay in getting that can out of the fire and it would have blown up. It is definitely not for an inexperienced cook."

Scott turned his attention to doing some cooking himself, and when they were filled with expertly bleeped food, they both lay on their sleeping bags, watching the campfire and starlit sky. Scott thought contentedly, "This is a lot like a nice little camping trip."

"Ken, do you know the name of the lookout we flew over a few minutes before we jumped today?" Scott asked.

"Yes, it's Sheepeater Lookout, named after the Sheepeater Indians that used to roam through this country," Ken answered.

"That's an unusual name for a tribe of Indians. I had never heard of them before you mentioned them that one day," Scott said.

Ken leaned forward, obviously very interested in this topic.

12

HISTORY UNFOLDS

"Sheepeaters is an unusual name, all right, but they were an unusual and unique tribe of Indians," Ken said.

"They lived in this rugged area?" Scott questioned.

"Yeah, they did, and they're the most fascinating group of people I've ever studied," Ken continued. "They were related to the Shoshone tribe, and their history goes back to ancient times." His face lit up as he continued with increasing enthusiasm. "They were named Sheepeaters by the early white men who came to this country in search of gold, because these Indians were skillful hunters and much of their diet was mountain sheep. As white men moved west in the late 1800's, some of the strong-spirited members of various tribes refused to go to reservations, so they fled to this isolated part of the United States and joined the Sheepeaters. The result was a band of Indians from all kinds of tribes and backgrounds who shared a common need to continue living in freedom. They were magnificently independent and developed unusual survival skills for living in such an inhospitable land."

"So the Sheepeater tribe grew as it took in the Indians from other tribes who refused to go with their own people to reservations?" Scott said, pondering the strength of their convictions.

"Yep, that's right," Ken answered.

Scott was fascinated and he waited quietly as Ken became more involved in telling the Sheepeater story.

"The U.S. Cavalry fought their last official Indian campaign against these Indians. Back in 1878 some settlers in Long Valley were killed, and the Sheepeaters were suspected. So, the U.S. Army decided to break the spirit of this group who had resisted their military authority for so long. They planned to drive them onto reservations, much as they had done a year earlier with Chief Joseph and the Nez Perce Indians. But the Army repeated the mistakes of the Nez Perce campaign, and underestimated both this rugged country and the spirit of these people."

"To make a long story short," Ken continued, "A number of armies chased the Sheepeaters all over this backcountry for two years, occasionally getting close enough for a skirmish. Finally, in 1879, they captured a few members of the band and took them off to reservations. The frustrated army had saved face and they dropped the campaign.

"The names of the Sheepeater chiefs fascinate me," Ken added. "War Jack, Eagle Eye, and Chuck. Chuck — now isn't that some name for a war chief?" Ken laughed.

Respect for these noble Indians shone in Ken's eyes and Scott suddenly understood what their lifestyle represented to his partner. The proud, strong spirit of the Sheepeaters was with them as Ken's reverent voice made history come to life. Scott could imagine War Jack, Eagle Eye, and Chuck moving in spirit through their homeland, the very place where Ken lay telling of their gallant last-ditch effort to remain free.

"You remember flying over the long sand bar near the place where Big Creek empties into the Middle Fork of the Salmon

River?" Ken asked. "It's called Soldier Bar on the map."

"Yes," Scott said, recalling the time Wayne Garrison had pointed it out to him.

"Well, some day you'll probably be on a fire in that area, and you can walk over and see the monument that the U.S. Army erected in honor of the soldiers who died in the Sheepeater Campaign of 1878-79," Ken said, his voice hardening. "It's a five-foot-high cone of boulders laid in cement with a marble headstone on top. The army hauled this monstrosity seventy miles by wagon and forty miles by pack mule to erect it in this remote area. A true monument to man's stupidity," Ken noted reflectively. "You must go see it."

As he looked into the dying embers of the campfire, Ken's voice was quiet, but intense. "You know I think our culture could learn a lesson or two from the Sheepeaters."

"How's that?" Scott asked sleepily.

"In modern America it seems unnecessarily hard for young people to pass from childhood to full adult membership in our society. There is no time schedule or set rules. I feel this creates confusion and vague expectations, causing a lot of problems for kids," Ken said.

"I haven't given it much thought, but that sounds right to me," Scott agreed.

Ken continued, "The Sheepeaters had a ceremony called a 'vision quest' that marked a teenager's passage into the adult world. Under the sponsorship of a tribal elder the adolescent underwent isolation and physical hardship. The plan was to bring on a trance and a visit from the Atutelary Spirit. This spirit would give the youth his song and instruct him in the purpose

91

for his life. From that day on he would experience all the privileges and responsibilities of an adult, clear and simple."

"That would make it easier," Scott answered.

"Sometimes I imagine that I can feel the spirit of those noble Indians," Ken added. "I can sense their courage and strength when I'm in this country."

As Scott drifted on the edge of sleep, he too could feel the presence of this spirit Ken spoke of.

The next day Scott and Ken got up early and began to finish up the fire. They cut down two trees with the misery whip.

"I can hardly straighten out my fingers, and look at those blisters!" Scott complained as he looked at his hands.

"Being a misery whip operator is hard work all right. I've picked up a few blisters myself," Ken agreed. "But your back and legs are all you'll need for tomorrow's packout," he added, as if he knew something Scott didn't.

The two jumpers cooled the logs with dirt until they could run their hands over every inch of them without feeling a warm spot. The last smoke was put out at 1300 hours. They knew that if they didn't see more smoke, it would be safe to leave the following morning.

"I am convinced that this fire is out," Ken said as he set about planning their next move. "KOD72, KOD72," he called into the hand-held short-wave radio. "KOD72, this is Beaver Creek smokejumpers," he continued.

"Go ahead Beaver Creek smokejumpers, this is KOD72," the dispatcher's voice cracked.

"We are ready to de-man the Beaver Creek fire and request further instructions."

"Stand by," the radio replied.

"10-4," Ken responded. As he waited, he told Scott, "That tops off a beautiful little fire. Perfect radio communication with the dispatcher in McCall—that's almost unheard of."

"Beaver Creek jumpers, Beaver Creek jumpers, this is KOD72," Ken answered.

"Instructions for de-manning Beaver Creek fire are as follows: Contour mountain going east for approximately one and one-half miles until you intersect with Hand Creek Trail. Wait for packer at this point on Hand Creek Trail. When the packer arrives, proceed north to Chamberlain Basin Landing Strip. A plane will arrive at Chamberlain Airstrip approximately 1700 tomorrow to return you to McCall."

"Message clear," Ken said into the radio.

"KOD72 out," was the farewell message from civilization.

"Beaver Creek jumpers out," Ken signed off, leaving the two jumpers once again in their beautiful, silent isolation.

The daylight was almost gone as Scott pulled the map from his pack and Ken joined him in checking on the route they would take out. They first clarified their present location, which was approximately a mile and a half from Hand Creek Trail and roughly fifteen miles from the Chamberlain Basin Landing Field.

"Don really had our position pegged when he turned in his report to the dispatcher," Ken said. "Wish he could have arranged us a helicopter ride to Chamberlain Basin though. No!" Ken corrected himself. "On second thought, I'd rather walk out of here than destroy part of the timber to make a landing pad for the copter."

"Some people would give most anything for an outing like this one we're getting paid for," Scott said. "These small fires are great."

"Wish they could all be like this," Ken said, knowing full well that the summer ahead would hold a lot of hard work. They lay back in their bedrolls in the flickering light of the campfire.

"How many years have you been smokejumping?" Scott asked Ken.

"Eight," Ken said, as if he couldn't quite believe it had been as long. "It's been a good job and it's put me through college."

"It's great you are still able to get away from your job each summer for a couple of months," Scott said.

"That's only one of the good things about being a school counselor," Ken agreed. "I like that job, too. One more summer after this and I plan to give this smokejumping business over to you young fellows," he added laughingly. "You know, I'm already thirty-two years old. I want to spend more time with my family and leave this hazardous stuff to you single guys."

"How many jumps do you have?" Scott asked.

"Ninety-three. When I've earned my hundred-jump pin I plan to hang it up," Ken said reflectively. "I should get it easily by next summer."

Feeling very comfortable with Ken, Scott inquired, "Does jumping out of airplanes get any easier after you've been around awhile?"

"Practice jumps and fire jumps with open landing areas do," Ken answered. "I know a lot more about jumping than I did when I started, and I've seen some unusual things happen to smokejumpers. I can probably foresee a lot of hazards that you're not aware of at this point. Sometimes more information can make it more scary, but the blind fear of the long step from the airplane is pretty much gone. Don't feel bad if it scares you. The guy I would worry about is the one who says jumping out of airplanes doesn't scare him. He's either crazy or stupid, and neither one of those characteristics make for a very good jump partner," Ken smiled reassuringly.

The fire died down to glowing coals and the stars shown brightly as Ken once again began to talk of his favorite subject, the inhabitants of the Idaho wilderness. He told stories of the hearty mountain men who were still living isolated lives in this country. Like the Sheepeater Indians before them, some of the present-day mountain men had come to this primitive country to escape the confines of a continually shrinking, overcrowded world. Others, Ken was sure, came because they were running from the law.

"Boy, would I like to run into a real mountain man while we're back here," Scott told Ken.

"Well, Buckskin Bill is the only one of the bunch that won't run like a deer at the sight of an outsider."

"Yeah? Tell me about this guy."

"That's a good story, but a long one," Ken said in a voice heavy with sleep. "What say we save it for another time?"

"OK," Scott agreed reluctantly, "But it's Buckskin Bill I want to see."

Looking into the glowing coals of the fire, Scott began to drift somewhere in that area between wakefulness and sleep. His mind was filled with thoughts about the Sheepeater Indians and the mountain men. It was evident to Scott that Ken admired the free spirit of both the Sheepeaters and current-day mountain men. In his drowsiness, Scott imagined a mysterious link of courage connecting these free-spirited people from the past to Ken — yes, to Ken and other freedom-loving people.

For a few fleeting moments as Scott hovered on the threshold of sleep, the world made sense and he was aware of a link across time.

13

HOME AGAIN, GONE AGAIN

Morning broke clear and bright. Ken and Scott ate before starting their packout. "A hundred-and-sixty pound man is just not meant to pack a hundred-and-five-pound pack around the side of a steep mountain without a trail," Scott told himself. Every step and every log crossing was a struggle. The trail was a welcome sight and the jumpers stacked their packs beside it, drank deeply from their canteens, and lay back in the shade to recuperate and wait for the packer and his mules.

After they had waited thirty minutes, they began to discuss the possibility of leaving their packs on the trail and starting their walk to Chamberlain Basin. No decision was necessary, however, because they heard the sound of the stock animals, and then the packer appeared around the corner of the trail riding a brown saddle horse, followed by two mules.

"Hello, Ed," Ken greeted the packer warmly.

"Guess I would have only needed one mule," Ed said as he looked at the two packs at the edge of the trail.

"Give 'em a break," Ken said. "I wouldn't ask a mule that I liked to pack two of those things."

"I can't believe they expect you guys to carry these," Ed said as he strained to lift one end of the pack onto the mule's back while Scott pulled on the other end. Ed told the two jumpers about the personalities of the mules he had chosen for this trip. "Now take Big John! This big guy has a mind of his own. It takes a lot of mule skinner talk to keep him in line. Edna, she always accepts her pack without a complaint," Ed said. "She likes to please and is always anxious to work. Big John just looks for ways to get out of it," Ed added.

"Wish I had some extra horses for you guys to ride," Ed said as he swung up into his saddle.

"Don't worry about it," Scott replied. "Without that pack, I'll be hard to hold down."

Ed rode out front and the jumpers followed the mules. After a couple of miles, the trail began to climb a steep grade. Ed stopped his horse, looked over his shoulder, and said, "You can hold onto Edna's tail going uphill if you want some help. But I wouldn't grab onto Big John's tail. He might boot you clean past Chamberlain Basin."

Scott had lost track of the time and distance as they waded across streams and traveled over mountains. Then, topping a ridge, Scott saw before him a mountain meadow with a wind sock at one end. "This is it! Chamberlain Basin Landing Strip, heart of the Idaho wilderness!" Scott declared. Nestled in the trees to the west of the runway was the Forest Service guard station, home of Ed, Edna, Big John, and a few of their friends.

"What a day!" Scott sprawled on the grass under a pine tree and pulled his logging boots from his hot, sweat-soaked socks. In spite of his tiredness, Scott felt a sense of relief and satisfaction.

"Would my dad love this country!" Scott told Ken. "He's read about the hunting and fishing out here."

"Yep, him and a lot of other people," Ken said. "More folks are coming here all the time." He paused for a moment and allowed his eyes to slowly scan the surroundings. "But, as you can see, population isn't a problem here yet." He waved his arm toward the solitude of the little Forest Service camp.

"You'll probably come out here on work projects some time. We often work trails, repair fences, and do general work around the guard station when we have a slump in the fire season. We usually stay right over there," Ken said, pointing to a row of tents set in a lodgepole thicket. "There is no mechanized equipment allowed here and no electricity, of course. The work is done by hand or with the use of mules and horses. Airplanes are the only motor-driven things allowed here. Gosh! I love this country," Ken said sincerely.

"It sure is peaceful," Scott agreed.

"Yeah, I would like to live at a station like this for a summer; bring my wife and kids and settle in for three months," Ken said wistfully. "We could spend the whole summer fishing the lakes and streams around here."

"I know one kid that would enjoy seeing this area and that's my kid brother, Jeff."

"Tool shed, blacksmith shop, and wood sheds; how self-sufficient this little outpost seems! It is as if history has been turned back and here I sit," Scott thought to himself in disbelief.

Right on schedule, the Twin Otter arrived for the trip back to

McCall.

As the plane flew over the primitive country, Scott realized that like the Sheepeaters and mountain men before him he had been touched by the spirit of the Idaho wilderness. The land of Eagle Eye, War Jack, and Chuck, the Sheepeater chiefs was like a dream lingering in his mind.

When the Twin Otter landed in McCall, Don Lent was waiting at the airport to take Scott and Ken back to camp. "Am I glad to see you two," Don welcomed them. "Camp has been cleaned out for the past two days."

"Must have really been some lightning storm that passed over the other night," Ken observed.

"Yeah, it sure was. You two will go back on the jump list as numbers three and four," said Don.

"That sounds good, but I hope we're around long enough to get a good night's sleep," Ken said.

"And a shower," Scott joined in.

"I've ordered a DC-3 and sixteen smokejumpers from Missoula, Montana, to serve as a backup crew," Don informed them, "and we should start getting our own men back by tomorrow afternoon."

"When do you expect the Missoula crew to arrive?" Scott asked.

"It looks like they'll be in first thing tomorrow. It seems the southern end of their territory got hit by the same storm we had," Don replied.

When they reached camp they unloaded their dirty and disorganized equipment at the fire cache and gave Don their fire report. Then Scott and Ken prepared for their next call. Once things were back in a state of readiness, Ken started over the hill to where he lived with his family in a trailer house furnished by the Forest Service.

"See you tomorrow!" Scott shouted after him.

"OK, jump partner!" Ken answered back as he disappeared into the trees.

"Jump partner," Scott thought to himself. "I'm really a smokejumper." Tired as he was, a feeling of pride flashed through him. Then he moved up the dirt path through the lodgepole pines to his barracks.

The building was quiet. The empty cots looked very military with blankets spread tightly over the thin mattresses, and then he saw that Guy's bed had clothes strewn around it, and the bulky outline of a body showed under the blankets. "Guy and Jack must have beaten us back to camp," Scott reasoned.

"What are you doing in bed so early?" he asked when Guy rolled over and looked at him.

"I'm too tired to talk about it," he said, closing his eyes and rolling over again.

The shower relaxed Scott, and he could hardly remember going to bed.

It seemed like he had just lain down when the light clicked on and Wayne was shaking him awake. "Ken and Jack will meet you two in the kitchen for breakfast, then we have a fire to check out," Wayne said as he turned and left.

Scott and Guy groped sleepily around for clean clothes and silently moved toward the lights of the kitchen. Ken sat at a table looking clean and renewed from his night's sleep. He greeted

101

Guy and Scott across fried eggs and hash browns. Scott wasn't hungry, so he helped himself to a glass of milk and stuck a couple of oranges into the pockets of his sweat shirt.

"What a packout we had," Guy said, stuffing food into his mouth. "It made our practice packout look like a picnic, Scott. I mean it! It really did!"

"We've got another little fire for your folks this morning," Wayne said.

"I like the sound of a little fire," Jack joined in, "but no long packouts, please," Jack added as he rubbed an apparently sore back.

"We had a long walk ourselves, didn't we, Ned Patrick?"

"Yep, it was plenty long enough for me," Scott agreed, hoping he would get the chance to tell Guy the whole story later.

Wayne said, "The lookout wasn't sure whether the fire would need two or four men, so we'll take you all out and have a look."

"Are the four of us the only jumpers in camp?" Ken asked.

"That's right, but the crew from Missoula should be in most any time."

Once at the airport and suited up, the jumpers loaded into the Turboporter, a plane with a single jet-prop engine that is located ahead of the wide square, overhead wings. It is an extremely modern and efficient aircraft that, like the Twin Otter, is ideally suited for backcountry bush-pilot type work. Wayne was in the co-pilot's seat as they rolled down the runway and slipped into the early morning sky. The Turboporter had lots of power, but it had limited space, so the four jumpers huddled close together as they sat on and around fire packs and equipment.

Climbing higher into the dawn, they headed north over the lake.

Ken pointed out a DC-3 with its red and green wing lights twinkling as it glided toward a landing on the runway they had just left. "There are the Missoula jumpers. They'll help us out until we get more of our own men back."

Conversation stopped, and one at a time the four jumpers nodded off to sleep as they sat crowded together in the plane. The Turboporter turned west to follow the Salmon River breaks and crossed Idaho's major north-south highway, which wound along the Little Salmon River. The tired jumpers slept soundly, unaware of the terrain below, as Wayne and Jerry's eyes searched the ridges and draws for smoke. They had been unable to locate the fire that War Eagle Lookout had reported, and the dispatcher in McCall requested that they fly a routine fire patrol pattern before they returned to McCall.

"That's the Rapid River drainage," Wayne pointed out.

"Do you know the name of every mountain and creek in the Payette Forest?" Jerry marveled.

"Well, I should, anyway," Wayne said modestly. "I've flown over them hundreds of times and been over most of this country on foot."

For the next two hours the Turboporter patrolled the west side of the Payette, looking for smoke. After inspecting the Hells Canyon and Seven Devils country carefully, Wayne radioed the dispatcher in McCall, "KOD72, KOD72, this is 68 Zulu, come in."

"This is KOD72, Go ahead 68 Zulu," the voice crackled.

"68 Zulu is leaving from Smith Mountain Lookout and

flying directly to McCall."

"10-4, 68 Zulu, will expect you to arrive McCall 0930 hours, KOD72 clear,"

"68 Zulu clear," Wayne answered as he removed the headset. "We should be back for coffee."

"Seems like it should be noon at least," Jerry said, "And here it isn't even 10 o'clock yet."

When the Turboporter cleared West Mountain, Jerry started his approach on the McCall runway.

"I hate to wake these turkeys up," Wayne said as he reached back from the co-pilot's seat to shake Ken. "They really look beat."

"Are we there?" Ken asked, straightening up and turning to look out the window.

"Dry run?" Wayne said.

"Dry run," Scott parroted, "What's that mean?"

"There's either no fire or we couldn't find it," Wayne said. "Sometimes lookouts see patches of low-hanging fog, or dust from a band of sheep and report it as a fire."

"Or the smoke may have just died down enough that we couldn't see it," Ken said. "If that's the case, we'll be back later."

"I could go for breakfast now!" Scott volunteered, glad they were back in McCall.

The jumpers piled out of the plane and began taking off the hot, uncomfortable suits. "It's a relief to get out of that thing and stretch," Scott said, as he stacked his parachutes and gear in a neat pile.

"Sure is," Guy agreed. "Do you suppose we can get Wayne to stop for donuts on the way back to camp?"

SMOKEJUMPER

A young man came out of the ready room with a note in his hand and gave it to Wayne.

Wayne read the note to himself, then called, "Put 'em on and load up."

"Really?" Scott heard himself saying in a whining voice, "And to think breakfast was so close."

The four jumpers suited up and reloaded into the Turbo-porter, and once again they started their flight north.

"The fire has been located this time," Scott thought when the pilot began circling over a ridge-top just north of the Salmon River.

Ken spoke up. "The Salmon River is called the 'River of No Return.' This is the river that forced Lewis and Clark to replan their route to the Pacific Ocean."

Wayne slid the huge door open and it was as if the entire left side of the airplane opened up. Scott clung to the side of the plane as far from the gaping door as he could get, then spotted the thin column of smoke War Eagle Lookout had reported. The fire was bigger than he had expected. A large blackened area was already visible on the ground. Apparently, the night air had slowed the fire's spread and made the smoke hard to find.

The jump spot was a clear pocket on the top of the ridge. Wayne timed the drift streamers to the ground and then held up four fingers, indicating he would put all four men on this one.

Jack and Guy, unable to straighten up in the small fuselage of the plane, moved to the door. They hooked the snap on their static-lines to the cable as they moved into position. Jack hung his feet out the door and slid his body forward until he was sitting on the very edge of the floor. Wayne lay in a cramped position back of the door. He could only see the ground by looking below Jack's legs as they extended out the door. Guy crouched behind Jack. A slap on the shoulder and Jack straightened his body and pushed off with his hands. He fell away into the morning air. Almost immediately, Guy duplicated Jack's exit. Wayne rolled the static-lines into the parachute covers and unhooked the static-line snaps.

Scott hooked up his own snap and cautiously eased himself into the gaping door. Sliding forward gingerly until he was sitting on the very edge, he held tightly to the door with one hand and gripped the floor with the other.

The pressure from the rushing air tried to force Scott's legs and feet back along the tail section of the fuselage. His heart pumped wildly as he strained to keep his balance. His mind was alert as he forced himself to concentrate on the jump spot that was rapidly approaching. The plane tilted slightly and Scott felt himself slipping off his perch. He gasped and tried to get steadied again just as Wayne slapped his shoulder and yelled, "GO!" Half falling and half jumping, Scott tumbled from the door. His legs came up and he fell away from the plane on his back. He had closed his eyes tightly for a fraction of a second, and when he opened them again, he saw the parachute lines whipping wildly from the tray on his back. They made a hissing, rubbing sound against the back of the high collar on his jump jacket. Once the lines were straight, the orange and white nylon broke away from the bag that held it, blossoming into its full glory in the morning sun.

"What a beautiful sight," Scott thought as he dangled beneath the brightly colored canopy.

SMOKEJUMPER

Scott turned his parachute in the direction of the two chutes settling into the clearing below.

Scott and Ken landed near each other. The morning air had given them a slow ride down and a soft landing.

The smoke pouring up from the fire burned in Scott's nostrils as he worked to shed his jump gear.

14

NORTH AMERICAN WAPITI

The Turboporter's first cargo pass dropped a bundle of fire-fighting gear in the clearing near the four orange and white para-chutes. The wind caught the white cargo chute and dragged the bundle ten yards across the ground before Jack grabbed the lines and collapsed one side of the billowing chute. "That ground wind is picking up," Ken said as he held his hard hat to his head. "It's a good thing we got here early."

The roar of the Turboporter sounded again, indicating that the second fire pack had been dropped. This time the ground wind grabbed the cargo chute and directed it into a tall fir tree that stood to one side of the clearing.

The shadow of the plane moved across the ground a final time, and looking up, Scott saw a small parachute with a foot-long package fall into the clearing. Then the plane dipped one wing and then the other as Wayne waved from the open door as if to say, "Sorry we put your cargo in a tree."

Scott walked to where the small package lay in the clearing and picked up the lineman's climbers they would need to get the cargo down.

"We have enough tools in this pack to get started," Ken said. "I don't want this wind spreading the fire all over the mountain while we're trying to get the rest of the cargo down."

SMOKEJUMPER

The four jumpers took hand tools from the pack, spaced themselves across the top of the fire, and began digging a fire line around the point of the spreading blaze. The wind was blowing the smoke up the mountain. Scott began coughing and his eyes were watering, so he stopped and tied a handkerchief across his face as he saw Jack and Ken doing. He closed his eyes to narrow slits and worked fast, trying to finish the line and get out of the heat and smoke. Occasionally, Scott moved out of the smoke for a couple of minutes and then charged back in for another try at controlling the blaze. After an hour and a half of battle, the point of the fire was capped and its rapid spread stopped.

"Scott and I will dig the fire line down the east side; Jack, you and Guy work down the west side," Ken directed.

Both teams worked quietly, digging and chopping a trench down each side of the fire.

"That sun is murder," Scott said, stopping for a moment. He was sweating heavily.

"Sure is," Ken answered, "but it looks like Jack and Guy are about to reach the bottom of the fire, too."

"Let's take a water break," Jack called out from across the fire.

"OK, that sounds good to me," Scott yelled back as he dropped into the shade of a pine tree.

The four tired fire fighters talked very little as they rested in the cool shade.

"If we dig a roll trench straight across this lower end of the fire, we'll have the whole thing tied in," Ken said looking relieved.

"Yeah, unless we get some strong winds we'll have this baby pretty well closed down," Jack assured them.

A roll trench across the bottom of a fire is much deeper than the line dug on the sides. It is designed to keep logs, pine cones, and hot rocks from rolling out the bottom of the fire.

The finish now in sight, the four jumpers worked with renewed strength. Soon the roll trench was completed and the blaze was completely circled.

"This baby isn't going nowhere," Jack proclaimed as he removed the last shovelful of dirt from the trench and sat down heavily with a sigh.

"Let's cool off that corner and get started on some dinner," Ken said, starting to move toward the southwest section of the fire.

"Almost 1800 hours. Looks like we've nearly put in a day."

"When the day starts before daylight you might say we have," Jack said wearily.

The four men spaded up dirt and covered the fallen logs that lay burning in a pile. Quickly the flames were knocked down and the southwest corner of the fire began to cool. Scott knew that burying the logs was only a temporary solution, for buried logs and roots can hold heat for days. They would have to be uncovered later and the burning coals scraped off.

The four men looked as if they had been wallowing in a coal bin as they moved their sweaty, tired bodies to the top of the ridge and began setting up a camp. Ken emptied out the fire pack. "We'll have to get the other pack out of that tree before dark," he said.

"Good thing we've got a couple of Neds with us to do that

sort of work," Jack chuckled as he cleared a bare spot on the ground to build a campfire.

"Yeah, we get the picture," Guy said, taking the climbers out of the canvas bag. "Scott, grab a let-down rope and let's show these old-timers how quickly we can get that cargo out of the tree."

Ken reached into his personal gear bag and pulled out a couple of medium-sized onions. "I'll start dinner," he volunteered. "A couple of fresh onions, canned meat and vegetables, and you've got a gourmet stew. Add a few John Wayne crackers and we'll be eatin' high on the hog, so's to speak," he finished with a twinkle in his eyes.

"Ned Edwards, didn't you say it was your birthday today?" Jack asked, chewing casually on his usual wad of tobacco.

"Twenty-one big ones, as of today!" Guy answered.

Jack grinned. "Almost seems as if we ought to celebrate such a momentous occasion, Neddy-boy. Maybe we'll say the stew is in your honor and seat you at the head of the dinner table."

"I remember our last celebration," Scott said, thinking of the fight in Council.

"Enough sentimental hogwash," Ken directed. "You guys had better start retrieving your cargo, or you'll be celebrating by spending the night without sleeping bags."

At the base of the fir tree Scott and Guy decided, in true smokejumper fashion, who would don the climbers and go up the giant tree. Scott's coin turned up a head and Guy's a tail. The birthday boy would climb the tree and saw off limbs while Scott worked to assist him from the ground.

Guy sat at the base of the tree and strapped the climbers to his logging boots. It was evident that he was a good climber as he quickly scaled the hundred feet to where the cargo hung. He ran the strap around the tree and tied it back to his belt. Now he could lean out from the tree to reach the cargo and still have both hands free to work. Taking the let-down rope off his shoulder, he ran the loose end through the lines of the cargo chute, under a strap on the cargo, and then tied it back to the parachute lines. Next he threw the nested bundle of rope out from the tree and the single braid strung out to within seven feet of the ground.

"Go ahead and pull on the rope," Guy yelled down. Scott had to jump to reach the rope and then he pulled down. "Hold it there." Guy yelled again. With the weight off the cargo, he was able to unsnap the sling that held it to the chute. "You can turn loose," Guy said, and began lower the bundle in a pulley-like fashion.

The rope was only long enough to lower the bundle to within thirty feet of the ground, so Guy let it drop from that height. It hit the ground with a heavy thud. "Open it up and take the sleeping bags out," he called. "The water container may have broken and we don't want to sleep in soaked bags."

"It's OK," Scott yelled up toward the top of the tree. "The water containers didn't break!" He was relieved to know his bed was still dry.

Scott pulled on the let-down rope that hung from the cargo chute, and Guy sawed limbs until the parachute was freed. It was getting dark as they gathered the cargo chute and fire pack in their arms and joined the two figures sitting in the firelight.

"Good to see our Neds are back," Ken said to Jack. "I

112

thought for a while they had decided to sleep in that tree."

"WE'RE GETTING BETTER EVERY DAY, WE'RE GETTING BETTER IN EVERY WAY, Uncle Ken," the two Neds sang out in unison as they teased back.

Jack scolded, "You wiseacre Neds, just no respect any more." It seemed the craziness was catching.

The laughter eventually quieted as the four hungry jumpers prepared to eat.

"I checked the fire again while Ken was cooking," Jack reported. "It's looking good except for the southwest corner. There is still a lot of heat in there; we should check it again after dinner." Jack spit brown juice on the pine needles, and loaded another wad of tobacco into his mouth.

Scott was starved and Ken's cooking lived up to his claims. Their feast of stew and lemonade was one of the best meals of Scott's life, even though they had only vegetable cans to use both as bowls and glasses. After they had eaten, Ken moved over to the fire packs just beyond the firelight. He turned his back and lit a match. When he turned around again and walked back into the firelight, he held something glowing in his hands, smiling from ear to ear as he began to sing...

"Happy birthday to you!"

Jack joined in, but with some of his usual sarcasm still in his voice...

"Happy birthday to you!
Happy birthday Neddy Edwards!
Happy birthday to you!"

By the time the end of the song was reached, Scott was singing along. Surprised and laughing, Guy blew out the ring of small burning pitch sticks that Ken held before him. "You weird clowns," Guy said, looking both pleased and embarrassed by all the attention.

The birthday cake was a small, round pound cake that came canned with the fire rations. It was frosted with a thick layer of strawberry jam that held up the stick candles. Ken cut the cake in fourths; everyone laughed and talked at once as they polished off the cake in the festive firelight.

"I think we started too early this morning; this group is getting giddy," Scott laughed. Their tiredness soon took over, the laughter quieted down, and the men sat looking into the campfire.

"Jack and I will check out the lower corner of the fire," Ken said, bringing their thoughts back to their duty. "If we give a hoot, bring your shovels and come on down."

Attaching flashlights to their hard hats, the two moved down the mountain into the darkness. Scott and Guy rolled out their sleeping bags and sat down, but just as they got settled and comfortable, they heard a "H-o-o-o-t" sound coming from the bottom of the fire.

"Here we go again!" Scott moaned as he picked up his shovel, hard hat and flashlight. "If there's anything I don't want to do it's fight more fire tonight."

When they arrived at the bottom of the fire Ken said encouragingly, "A couple more hours of work tonight and we can save ourselves an extra day here."

"I'm still not sure it's worth it," Scott thought as he began digging up the logs they had buried earlier in the afternoon. Cooling and scraping, they worked in the heat for two hours.

Not a glowing coal was visible when the silent group was finished. Completely exhausted, they climbed the mountain to their camp and bedded down.

"Neds, don't wake me until the coffee's ready in the morning," Jack ordered drowsily from his sleeping bag.

Guy played his harmonica softly as he tried to relax his tense muscles. Scott was exhausted, but he felt a special closeness to the work team he had shared this long day with. Looking at the night sky, he thought, "Could these stars have looked any different to the Sheepeater Indians who once roamed this land so freely? This, too, is a part of the vast, wild country that was their home." He then drifted off to sleep.

It seemed only moments later that Jack shook Scott awake. "Hey, look at that!" Sleepily, Scott opened his eyes and searched the gray dusk of morning for whatever it was that had gotten Jack so excited. Then he saw them. Toward the lower end of the opening in the timber stood a big bull elk and two cow elk. Cautiously the animals moved across the opening. Guy and Ken were awake, too, and watched the elk intently. "They're downwind of us," Ken murmured. The bull raised his head and looked about alertly.

"What a majestic animal," Scott said under his breath. "He looks bigger than a horse, yet he moves like a graceful deer." Scott could see that his antlers were covered with velvet. The bull had five rounded points on each antler. He seemed to sense something wasn't right and moved with the two cows silently into the trees.

"North American Wapiti," Ken said with respect in his voice.

"What do you mean, Wapiti?" Guy asked sleepily. "I've seen

115

Toward the lower end of the opening in the timber stood a big bull elk and two cow elk.

those animals before, and they're elk."

"That's what they're typically called," Ken explained, "but the Indians called them Wapiti, meaning white rump, and that became their scientific name. Early white men called them elk because they looked somewhat like a European moose that was called an elk. It's a case of mistaken identity that just caught on. The last big herds anywhere in the world are found right here in Central Idaho. They are so sought after as trophy animals that this is one of the few areas left where they are able to survive in large numbers."

After drifting back to sleep, Scott awoke again as the sun broke into the eastern sky. "Was I dreaming or did I see some elk this morning?" Scott asked stretching his arms above his head.

"You weren't dreaming, but you weren't listening either," Ken answered back with a smile. "Those things you saw were Wapiti!"

"Wait until I tell my dad! He has been a Wapiti hunter all these years and didn't even know it." Scott said.

15

A LINK WITH THE PAST

The four smokejumpers spent a few minutes talking about the Wapiti and eating breakfast before they returned to the burned-over area of the fire. Ken had been right—the two hours of late-night work had cooled the fire and not a sign of smoke was visible as they spread out, digging and combing through the burn.

Guy was bent over a blackened log as he worked on a steep rocky part of the burn. "Oh, no!" he yelled suddenly, and began tumbling down the mountain-side. He stopped rolling when he hit an outcropping of rock.

"I'll be right there," Scott called as he moved quickly toward his friend, who lay stretched out on the ground. Guy was holding his left arm gingerly.

"Watch out," Guy warned as Scott approached. "There's a rattlesnake under that log!" Guy's face was drawn in pain.

Scott's eyes darted from bush to rock, chills running up and down his spine, feeling as if snakes could be attacking him from all directions.

"Ken, Jack, come quick!" Scott called out frantically as he tried to control his fear.

"Where were you bit?" Scott asked Guy, trying hard to sound calm.

With his face still tight from the pain in his arm, Guy managed a smile. "I didn't get bit," he explained. "I almost touched that rattler and when I saw how close to him I was, I lost my balance and fell. I skinned the hide off my arm on those rocks."

Ken and Jack ran over, looking alarmed because of Scott's cry for help. Guy repeated his explanation much to their relief. Then Ken washed Guy's arm and placed a sterile bandage over the broken skin.

"Rattlesnakes are dangerous anytime, but especially around a forest fire," Jack warned. "Sometimes they'll get burned, but not killed. Then with their rattlers burned off and blinded, they strike wildly at anything that gets close."

"This reminds me of a story about two back-packers," Ken said with a twinkle in his eye.

"I think we're gona hear about the two back-packers if we want to or not," Jack said setting down with a sigh.

Ken continued as if he hadn't heard Jack. "They were hiking along the trail when one of them got bit on the backside by a rattler. It seems his partner didn't know how to treat snake bite, so he hurried off to the nearest ranger station and called a doctor. He said, 'Doc you've gotta come quick! My friend has been bitten by a rattlesnake.'" Ken was excitedly into character.

Then in a deep doctor voice Ken answered himself, "I can't get there in time to save his life, but you can treat the snake bite yourself by cutting into the fang marks with your pocket knife and sucking out the poison."

"You don't understand!" Ken said resuming the high voice. "It's not that simple, he hasn't been bit on the arm or leg. He was bit right on the rump!"

"Well, if you're to save your buddy's life you'll just have to do it." Ken said in a deep voice.

Ken continued, "frantically this guy ran back up the trail to where his wounded buddy waited and said, 'I'm sorry but the doc can't come.'"

"Well, what did the doctor say?" Ken pleaded as the snake bitten man. "WHAT DID HE SAY?"

Looking sad and shaking his head slowly, Ken again answered as the friend. "Doc says you're gonna die!"

Ken slapped his knee and bent over in laughter. The others laughed too, not because the joke was funny but at Ken's absolute delight.

"This fire is out! Let's get out of here," Jack proclaimed.

Ken agreed. "We can catch a ride to Mackey Bar on the Forest Service jet boat that patrols the Salmon River."

"Luckily, the trail to the river isn't far from here," Jack added. "Let's get things ready to pack off."

After making a final check of the burn, the jumpers struggled to their feet with their heavy packs and headed toward the river.

"Boy, does this feel familiar," Scott said as his sore muscles began to complain.

"Yeah," Ken agreed. "I feel like a GS-7 Forest Service mule."

"Oh, come on," Jack said. "This packout can't possibly be as bad as our last one. Let's go before we talk ourselves out of it."

Jack led the way. Guy went next, then Ken, and Scott brought up the rear. In a short time they were at the river.

"Man, does that water look inviting," Jack said as they

dropped their packs in the sand. In a few minutes they were diving and swimming in the deep hole beside the sandy bank. The water felt great as they washed away the smoke and grit of the fire.

Cooled and relaxed by the water, the four naked bodies were lying on the white sand enjoying the sun's healing rays when a rubber raft rounded the bend in the river. Yelling and laughing, they scrambled for their Levis. "I'll bet they think they're seeing a herd of Wapiti," Guy laughed.

"At least they saw a herd of white rumps," Ken chuckled as the cheering boatload of tourists disappeared from sight.

About 1530 hours, the aluminum Forest Service jet boat came into sight and responded to the jumpers' frantic arm waving. "How are you doing, Burt?" Ken and Jack welcomed the boat as it nudged into the sandbar.

The driver was a small, fine-boned man with a weathered and salty look. He wore a green baseball cap and clenched a pipe in his teeth. Ken introduced Burt to the others, then they loaded their gear in the jet boat. Ken asked Burt, "Do you suppose Buckskin Bill will be home today?"

"I'll bet he is," Burt replied. "He was home yesterday when I made my trip."

"You mean we may see the famous mountain man?" Scott's voice showed his excitement.

"I hope so," Guy chimed in. "I've heard a lot about this hermit."

"Man! That would be great!" Scott said. "I can't believe it."

"Bill is a mountain man for sure, but he is no hermit," Burt said. "He loves people and he is glad to share his life with most everyone. But you can't get close to the other River Rats that live along this canyon."

"That's why Buckskin is so well known," Ken said. "The first time I saw him I couldn't believe my eyes. I was sure I had run into a guy who had been in hibernation for the last hundred years."

"I hope he's home," Guy said wistfully.

"With a little luck, we'll catch him there today," Burt said.

"If he isn't home, at least you'll see his place," Ken added.

Burt fired up the jet engine and they started into the rapids under full power, the boat bouncing and bucking. They were challenging the "River of No Return!"

Scott was amazed by the continuous white water of the Salmon. The fresh, clean water sprayed the crew and pounded at the hull of the boat.

"Did you see that?" Scott shouted as a startled mule deer flashed into the brush near the edge of the water.

"Watch to your left. There are usually mountain goats near the top of those cliffs," Burt said, nodding his head toward the rocky breaks rising straight up from the river. Burt's hands gripped the steering wheel, fighting to keep control of the boat.

They had been on the river for an hour when several old buildings came into view on the south bank. "This must be the home of the famous Buckskin Bill," Scott thought. The boat nosed into the bank in front of the buildings.

The small, weathered buildings were grouped at the base of a cliff where a stream ran into the river. A high fence enclosed a garden.

"That's to keep deer and other wild animals out of his

The sight took Scott's breath away as the mountain man walked toward him. (Drawing by Robert Auth)

vegetables," Ken explained.

An old man with a flowing, gray beard and a neatly trimmed moustache appeared from the direction of the creek. Buckskin Bill was every bit as colorful as Ken had described him, dressed in a fringed leather outfit, knee-high moccasins, and a fluffy bear-skin hat. He had a powder horn hung at his side and a long rifle cradled in his left arm. The sight took Scott's breath away as the mountain man walked toward him. "Where has this man been the last century?" Scott asked himself.

"Hi ya, Bill," Burt greeted him.

"Who ya got with ya today?" Bill asked.

"These young fellows are smokejumpers who dropped in on a fire upriver a piece," Burt answered.

"They're hitchin' a ride to Mackey Bar. Uncle Sam plans to pick them up and give them a plane ride back to McCall this evening."

"Glad you're going and not me!" Bill said to the jumpers. "I went to town a year ago and I haven't gotten over it yet. You boys got time for a cup of tea?" he asked politely. "I just got back from an afternoon hunt."

"I'm running late on this run," Burt said, "but these guys would like a tour if you wouldn't mind."

"Sure," Bill said, and like a tour guide, he showed them his elaborate garden and the machine shop where he had made the flintlock rifle which he used for hunting. Bill also showed them several knives he had made.

"What a craftsman," Scott said softly into Guy's ear.

"I didn't think you believed in machines and things like that," Jack said to Bill as he looked around the well-furnished, if not

124

modern, workshop.

"I have nothing against the use of machines," Bill said with conviction, "as long as I'm in charge of them and not the other way around."

Bill explained, "I was a mechanical engineer and lived pretty much like everyone else until I served a hitch in the army during World War II. When I got out of the service, I moved to this old mining claim." He proudly showed some more of his handmade rifles and some cougar embryos he had preserved in quart jars of alcohol.

All of the furniture was made from handhewn lumber, buckskin straps, and elk (or Wapiti) antlers.

Jack asked, "What is this?" as he pointed to an unusual window in one of the buildings.

"It is the plastic bubble off the front of a small World War II military plane," Bill answered. The four-foot high bubble had been built right into the south wall of the small stone structure.

"This man is ahead of his time," Scott thought to himself as he noted the solar heating potential of the window.

"I salvaged that from a wrecked plane I found a couple of miles from here," Bill said as they looked on in amazement.

In one cabin there were a number of cans of imported tea and stacks of magazines and books.

Hating to leave the serenity and Bill's hospitality, the travelers reluctantly said good-bye and loaded back into the jet boat. As he watched the strange figure waving from the bank, Scott knew that he had found a spirit who was somehow linked to the Sheepeaters of the past.

Several more miles downriver, the steep canyon walls parted slightly where the south fork of the Salmon joins the main Salmon River. At this wide place in the canyon Scott saw several cabins, a hunting lodge, and an airstrip just back from a natural sandbar.

"This is Mackey Bar," Jack said, jumping into the shallow water and beaching the boat.

They stacked their equipment alongside the short runway and headed for the lodge. After he had greeted the woman in the lodge, Ken asked, "Would you call the Forest Service in McCall and tell them that Ken Satterfield and his crew are here waiting for a ride back to McCall?"

"We might as well plan to eat dinner here at the lodge," Ken said. "The plane won't be in until later, anyway. You can only take off from these short runways when the air is cool and dense enough to give the plane maximum lift."

After dinner they sat in a circle, talking and playing cards. "The pine needles are worth a nickle each?" Scott asked, wanting to be sure of the rules.

"That's right, Neddy fish. Now throw in your bet," Jack said, trying to keep the poker game going. "I don't mind giving private lessons, but I like to make it worth my time, ya know." He lifted his head to spit some tobacco on the grass several feet away.

Standing up and moving toward the landing strip, Ken said, "You won't get much from these fish today, Jack. I hear the plane coming now."

Scott heard the Turboporter too as it descended over the south wall of the canyon, then dropped sharply, touching down on the small airfield. The props blew cards and pine needles in all directions.

"Too bad," Scott said with mock regret. "I guess there's no way now to tell who was winning. Right, Jack?"

"You Neds are a waste of time," Jack grumbled.

Jerry estimated the weight of each fire pack as he arranged them carefully and strapped them down in the plane. Then he looked over the four men and said, "We'll just figure you guys at two hundred pounds each. Now let's wait until it cools off a little more before we try to get out of this canyon."

Jerry joined the group as they resumed their card game. "I'll get some money out of you turkeys yet," Jack bragged.

"You bet," Guy harassed back. "We haven't seen anything but talk."

At dusk the five men loaded into the Turboporter. The take-off was much like being catapulted from an aircraft carrier. Jerry wound the engine up tight and they shot down the short runway. After climbing only twenty feet into the air, the plane sped out over the river. A hundred feet down the river a downdraft hit the left wing causing that side of the plane to drop suddenly. Scott's heart stopped as men and equipment were thrown against the walls.

"What is going on?" Scott thought in confusion.

Jerry quickly corrected for the sudden shift of the plane; then turned to Ken, who sat in the co-pilot's seat. "See why we waited that extra hour for the air to cool. The currents in this canyon are always unpredictable."

16

THE TRAVELING CREW

When the crew returned to McCall the fire bust was over. It had ended as quickly as it had begun, and the Missoula smoke-jumpers had already left for home. Most of them hadn't been on a fire during their stay in Idaho.

Scott was excited to see he had a letter from Julie, and he settled back to read it. He would have some time to catch up on his correspondence for the hectic pace would slow temporarily.

Scott, Guy and a few other men spent several days working on a new campground being constructed near McCall. To keep life interesting, a "heads out" contest was usually held to see who would buy the pop for afternoon break.

The mosquitoes were thick in the campground and one day Jack decided it was time to have a "Ned flip" (Neds only, old-timers excluded).

"The loser will stand motionless for five full minutes with his shirt off," Jack directed from his self-appointed position of authority.

"Neds only, that's not fair," Scott grumbled. "The whole idea stinks." He was disgusted at the thought of having anyone eaten alive by the swarming insects. Resentfully he joined in the flip.

Silver dollars, quarters, and nickels sparkled in the sunlight as they spun in the air and dropped to the dirt road. When a coin came up heads, the owner moved out of the circle. Those who flipped tails remained kneeling. Seeing the shiny face on his quarter, a relieved Scott stepped back from the circle.

His relief was short-lived, though, as a cheer went up, marking the end of the flip, and he saw that Guy was the loser.

At that moment Jack's face looked cruel and distorted as he chewed excitedly on his tobacco, proclaiming himself official timekeeper and said, "Strip to the waist N-e-d; this is going to be a really good s-h-o-w."

Guy removed his shirt and the insects swarmed onto his skin. Scott's own skin crawled at the thought of all the painful welts.

"This is ridiculous! Don't do it, Guy!" Scott called out realizing that he could not remain silent.

"Mind your own business, N-e-d-d-y Newman!" Jack taunted, giving Scott a push away from the circle of jumpers. "The Smokejumper Code will be upheld."

Something seemed to snap in Scott's head as the summer's harassment and Jack's mocking voice came together in an explosive mixture. Seeing red, Scott stepped boldly in front of the old-timer. His right hand started toward the tobacco juice dripping from the corner of Jack's mouth.

"Are you crazy?" Guy's voice boomed as he grabbed Scott's arm. "Jack's right, it's none of your business. Now cool off."

Scott's arm dropped to his side. He stepped across a fallen log and walked into the shade of the pine trees.

"A smokejumper has no honor if he won't carry through on a lost flip, and if he can't do it on his own, we'll hold him down twice as long," Jack snarled after him.

"Honor. That's a bunch of crap," Scott muttered through

clenched teeth as he stalked away.

"One minute!" The announcement was followed by a cheer.

There was a pause that seemed to hang in the silent air for ages; then came the announcement, "Two minutes!"

"This is ridiculous!" Scott grumbled to himself. His anger turned to sad amazement, and he walked over to a pile of brush and started to work. "At least I don't have to watch it," he said to himself.

"Five minutes! Hooray! He made it!" the group yelled and Scott knew Guy's ordeal was over.

"It's hard to believe," Scott thought.

Guy was working near Scott later in the day. "I can appreciate you speaking up for me this morning," Guy told him. "You should have known that one direct hit from those sledge hammer arms of Jack's and you would have gone to sleep early." Guy tried to make light of the situation, but the sincerity of his thanks came through clearly.

"You're right. It is kind of good to stay awake through the daylight hours. Besides, it really wasn't any of my business," Scott said, uncomfortable with the subject.

A week of working on the new campground and another lightning storm passed through. Scott and Guy rotated to numbers seven and eight on the roster, and any hope they had of having a free weekend in McCall began to fade.

Don Lent moved about the barracks with a flashlight, awakening smokejumpers. "Scott! Scott!" Don said, shaking his shoulder. "Bring your extra pack. You're going to Redmond,

Oregon for a while. They're having a real fire bust over there."
Don then moved on through the barracks, selectively awakening
the crew he needed.

With daylight breaking, the plane lifted off the runway and
headed west. Scott recognized Hells Canyon. So much had happened in the few weeks since he was here on the Brownlee Creek
fire.

"See that?" Scott asked, leaning toward Guy, who was shift-
ing awkwardly as he scratched his mosquito bites.

"That's where it all started," Guy said. "Sometimes I feel like
we may get more fires than we want before this summer's over."

Scott nodded yes as he admitted to himself for the first time
that he was tired.

"A day off would be nice," Scott said, leaning back against
the fuselage of the vibrating old plane.

The aircraft landed in sight of the Three Sisters Mountains.
Redmond was situated in the sagebrush flatlands and the smokejumper base had been built beside the runway.

The jumpers unloaded and joined with the others for an
orientation briefing in the loft building. They leaned on the
packing tables and sat on their gear bags, lining the walls.

"A lightning storm moved across Central Oregon yesterday.
We have seventy-four fires reported and we expect more. Most
of our men are already on fires. You guys from Montana,
Idaho, and Washington will be added to our jump roster," the
lanky foreman explained. He continued explaining local
procedures and how the massive assault on the forest fires would
be conducted. "OK, check out your living quarters," the
foreman ended his talk.

SMOKEJUMPER

Morale was high. The men laughed and talked as they looked for their names on the new jump list.

"Look! We're jump partners," Guy said. "I'm number forty-five and you're forty-six."

"You mean my J.P. is a mosquito-bitten Ned," Scott teased.

Many of the experienced jumpers knew each other from previous trips like this one. They swapped jump stories and recalled past fires they had shared from Southern California to the Bering Straights of Alaska.

Scott and Guy knew no one other than the McCall men they had arrived with, yet they felt the kinship these smokejumpers shared.

Scott was amazed by the way smokejumpers from all over the western United States could come together and work as a team. They could use any of the regional bases as their head-quarters. With the crews intermixed, the smokejumper's life could depend on men he had never met before. "That is the real contradiction in smokejumping; a high level of inter-dependence, plus an unusual amount of self-reliance," Scott thought.

The Redmond unit handled logistics well even though there were three times as many men as the center had been built to accommodate. The smokejumpers were constantly on call, ready to respond to a fire at any time. In small groups they worked on equipment and around the grounds. When the work was done, they had hard-fought volleyball or basketball games. Sometimes the men chose to conserve their strength and watched T.V., played poker, or just sat in the recreation room.

Jack soon found himself a place at the poker table. "You like to join the game?" he asked Scott. "You know I never finished your first lesson."

Scott didn't answer as he dropped into an easy chair.

"Suit yourself, Ned," Jack grinched.

In Redmond the fire call was a siren followed by a loud-speaker calling out the names of the jumpers who were to suit up and load into the waiting plane. This siren sounded frequently during the day, sending men scrambling, and moving Scott and Guy higher on the jump roster. Jumpers were also returning from fires continually. They cleaned up their equipment and then placed their names on the bottom of the list.

Several of the men in the rec room had fought forest fires in Alaska. Scott listened eagerly as they told their stories.

"Alaska sounds exciting. I can't wait to get sent on a fire up there," Scott told Guy excitedly.

"Sounds scary to me," Guy volunteered.

"Ring, r-i-n-g," the dinner bell sounded, interrupting Scott's thoughts about the northern slopes of Alaska. After dinner a helicopter landed with a Redmond jumper strapped in one of its side baskets.

"His leg is broken and he dislocated his shoulder," a squad leader from Redmond reported. "They tell me his chute pulled loose, and he fell out of the tree." Scott watched as they loaded him into the waiting ambulance.

After another day of stand-by, Scott and Guy's fire call came. "I feel a bit funny," Scott said as he prepared to load into the plane. "You and I are the only two McCall jumpers going on this fire," he told Guy.

Scott was aware of tension in his stomach. "But isn't loading into an airplane for the purpose of parachuting into a forest fire in tall timber reason enough to have a tight stomach?" he asked himself.

Trying to calm down, Scott recalled Ken's words, "If a person can do this kind of work with no fear he is either stupid or crazy." The knot in Scott's stomach reassured him that he was neither.

The fire was consuming brush and yellow pine trees when they arrived. The sagebrush clearing the spotter had chosen for their drop zone was filled with logging slash and stumps.

"Wish Ken was spotting!" Scott said in Guy's ear.

"Yeah, anyone from McCall would be all right with me," Guy answered.

The first two smokejumpers to exit the plane hit in the trees to the north of the spot. The next two landed too far south. By the time Scott stood in the doorway he could see that only three out of the ten parachutes had reached the ground. The others hung in tall trees. "I wish I had more confidence in the spotter or myself," Scott thought as he felt the knot in his stomach grow and weakness spread over his body. The air rushing past the plane seemed to sense his fear; it tugged at his suit, hissed in his ears, and stung his eyes.

He felt the spotter's hand hit his leg and he stepped out the door. Guy followed one step back. Both jumpers worked their chutes desperately, fighting for the clearing. They hit it, landing less than ten yards apart.

"I guess that proves who trains the best chute handlers," Guy smiled with relief as he pulled off his helmet and pointed it toward the parachutes in the trees.

134

"I guess that shows how well we can work these chutes when we're scared," Scott disagreed.

"We know that, but let's not tell them," Guy said, motioning toward the others. "Let's let them think we do it all the time."

The roads and flatness of the terrain made it possible to bring in ground crews a short time after the jumpers landed. A large camp was set up, and a bulldozer was brought in to work the lower part of the fire. The blaze was contained by 1900 hours and the jump crew was released from the fire line. They walked to base camp, washed, and got in line for dinner.

"How hot has it been today?" Scott asked a man serving in the chow line.

"A little over a hundred degrees," the man answered.

"It feels like it," Scott agreed. "I'm really wrung out."

After dinner the jumpers returned to the fire to ignite the unburned patches of fuel inside the line. By morning the crew was exhausted and they were glad to be sent back to base camp for breakfast. The fire was now controlled and plans were made to release them.

When the bus unloaded at the Redmond smokejumper base, it was obvious that the fire bust of three days before was now over. The long row of jumper planes were gone, and only a couple of aircraft remained on alert.

"Yes, I'm ready to return to McCall," Scott thought to himself as Guy went to check in with the office.

"The rest of our McCall crew has already gone," Guy reported. "They said as soon as we clean up and get our gear together, that Cessna Sky Wagon will take us back to McCall. Things are happening in McCall—that's why our crew was called back before we were all gathered up."

Scott's eagerness to get back to McCall was tempered by dismay at the prospects of having to go on another fire as soon as they arrived home.

"Hey, J.P." he said to Guy, "I sure am getting tired out. I could do with a little fishin' time. How about you?"

Guy responded with mock seriousness. "None of that complaining, Ned. Remember — you hired on to be tough!"

17

THE GOBBLER

The base at McCall was nearly deserted; twenty men had gone to Fairbanks, Alaska, shortly after Scott's group had left for Oregon.

"We missed this one," Scott moaned when he found out about the Alaska trip.

"Yeah, but we'll get there eventually," Guy said, feeling disappointed too.

Some of the other jumpers were on small fires near McCall, leaving Scott once again near the top of the jump list. He wearily realized that he hadn't had a day off for nearly a month, and he knew it could be some time before he would. Water skiing, beach parties, and weekend backpacking trips into remote, trout-filled lakes would have to wait for a more normal fire season. Rumor had it that if the pace held, this could be a record-breaking summer for forest fires.

Scott was relieved when Don Lent said, "Take care of your laundry and personal business; then get some rest."

Relaxing in the barracks, Scott learned that some of the crew had made a rescue jump while he was in Oregon. A small plane with four people aboard had hit the top of a mountain near Indian Creek. Chuck and three others parachuted in beside the crash to provide first aid and to make a helicopter spot so the survivors could be airlifted out.

After dinner Scott fell asleep in the shade of the loft building.

"B-u-z-z-z-z-z!" The sound of the alarm brought Scott to his feet, confused and half asleep. The short blasts seemed to continue endlessly as he raced to the fire cache and grabbed his gear. Men were running from every direction.

When the jumpers reached the airport, the props were turning on both the DC-3 and the Twin Otter. On the other side of the runway the modified World War II bombers were being loaded with fire retardant as their noisy engines belched fire and smoke.

"This fire must be a real gobbler!" Ken said. "Look at all the excitement."

They packed into the Twin Otter and were on their way. The DC-3 took off directly behind them and trailed them north toward the Salmon River breaks.

A turbulent cloud of dark smoke was seen long before the Salmon River was visible.

Off to one side of the billowing cloud of smoke, the jump planes began to circle. They waited and watched as the bombers dived repeatedly into the smoke, dropping thousands of gallons of liquid fire retardant onto the flames.

Tony sat at the open door. He was leaning out over the strap that blocked it. "What an air show!" he shouted as his hair and moustache blew in all directions.

A helicopter sat down on a ridge across from the fire. It would wait there until the smokejumpers had jumped and then it would begin to ferry men from the nearest road to the open side

138

of the fire. It was late evening and the wind was letting up.

With his heart pounding once again, Scott began moving through the routine he had been so thoroughly taught in training: helmet and gloves on, tighten leg straps, hook up static-line, safety pin in, check jump partner. With all these things running through his head, he had little time to worry about what waited on the ground below. With each circle of the plane, two smokejumpers stepped out, leaving more room inside. With each pass, Scott and Guy moved closer to the vacuum-cleaner door that continued to suck their buddies into the sky.

Scott stood in the open door of the plane. Ken was the spotter and he described the wind direction, the landing spot, and how the jumpers were to group up for their attack on the raging fire once they were on the ground.

"The jump spot is a good distance from the blaze, but use your head! That fire's coming fast! The wind currents are unstable! Don't take any chances!" Ken shouted his last-minute advice above the noise of the open door.

Stepping into position, Scott looked at the flames consuming the trees and brush, orange fingers flickering into the evening air. He clenched his teeth, forcing air through his nostrils and stiffening every muscle against the now familiar weakness in the pit of his stomach.

Scott was frightened by the jump, but the sight of the wild fire raging below sent an even greater, more instinctive fear through him.

"What if I get twisted? What if I get twisted and can't guide my chute?" The thought flashed like a red warning light in Scott's head. "What if..."

The slap on the back of Scott's left leg came and his breath stopped as he fell toward the flames and boiling smoke. Scott helplessly waited until he felt the tug of the parachute taking air.

Quickly, he checked his chute and saw the beautiful orange and white circle above his head. The lines hung straight down from the canopy. "I'm not twisted," Scott sighed with relief. He began working toward the jump spot, then realized that he had missed the opening on the ridge. He would have to turn back or land a mile down the mountain. Scott pulled the left guideline and the chute responded quickly.

Scott was sweaty and winded by the time he had packed his gear back to the ridge.

Wayne and Chuck directed the crew to stack their gear on a rocky outcropping and to shovel dirt over it. "In this country a man can have enough trouble keeping himself out of the fire without worrying about his equipment," Chuck warned.

"I talked with the fire boss on the radio and he said that before morning, crews brought in by helicopter would be working up from the bottom," Chuck told the jumpers.

It was dark now and they attached flashlights to their hard hats and took extra food and water. Chuck started the second planeload of jumpers down the east side of the fire, while those in Scott's unit started digging a fire line down the west side.

The crew laughed and talked excitedly as they walked nearer the uncontrolled flames. Some jumpers were again giving Hardluck the business telling him, "It's your fault we're on this monster."

140

"Get off my case," he answered good naturedly.

Approaching the fire, they saw that the cool night air was slowing the blaze. Even so, the heat forced them to leave more unburned material between the flames and themselves than they would have liked.

There was no talk now as the crew seriously performed the job they were trained for. Like a long snake, the twelve jumpers chopped roots and limbs and tore at grass sod. They left a trail behind them a foot wide and six inches deep.

Sweat rolled down Scott's face as he struggled with the noisy, vibrating chainsaw.

About midnight Wayne said, "Let's bleep some chow and take a break." There was little conversation and most of the men were too tired to eat. They fell asleep leaning against trees or sprawled in the freshly cut fire line.

"Glamorous job all right," Tony said, looking at the collapsed bodies.

Scott huddled near a burning log. Then he dozed off, only to be awakened by the heat on his face and the freezing stab of the cold night air down his back. He lay there half awake, feeling jumpy, thinking of the many times men working above him had yelled, "R-o-c-k!" sending him scurrying for a tree or cliff to hide behind. He would wait there until the rock had crashed past, or a second call announced that the rock had stopped.

When Scott saw Wayne get to his feet, he knew the break was over. Wayne picked up his pulaski (pickax) and started marking the course for the firebreak. The tired crew resumed work, straining to see in the glow from the fire and the washed-out

141

light of their headlamps. Scott's back was stiff and the blisters on his hands ached. The fingers on his right hand cramped on the chainsaw handle, and he had to use his left hand to release them. He realized it was time to trade for another tool.

At daybreak the crew stopped work for an hour and tried to get comfortable enough to sleep on the steep hillside.

"How can it be so hot during the day and so blasted cold at night?" Guy wanted to know.

"Beats me!" Scott said sleepily as he pulled the hood up on his sweatshirt, realizing there was no way he could keep warm.

The fire they had worked so hard to suppress seemed to have given up, except for an occasional flare-up and the glowing coals.

"Looks like we'll be off this little honey by this afternoon," Hardluck said.

"Don't count these Salmon River fires out too easily," Wayne warned. "It may look like it's about out, but the afternoon winds do some tricky things in this country."

At 0900 hours they stopped again and ate some canned fruit. Scott's eyes grew heavy and he slipped into a deep sleep, grateful for the warmth of the morning. Later he awoke with his mouth as dry as cotton, his body sweating from the traitorous sun that was no longer warm, but cruelly hot.

His eyes were matted from the smoke and irritation.

He opened his eyes and the psychedelic colors of the direct sunlight slammed against his brain. Scott's head ached and his right leg had gone to sleep. He stumbled into the shade of a pine tree and drank the warm water from his canteen.

He began to revive and watch the others seek the shade as he had done. "I feel like something bad's had a hold of me," Scott complained to Wayne.

"You think you feel bad, you should see what you look like," Wayne answered.

"Well, don't blame me for it," Hardluck grumbled.

Looking up the mountain, Scott could see that yesterday's wild fire was now controlled on all sides. Focusing his vision to the north, he saw the beautiful 'River of No Return' stretched out before him. Their night's work had brought them to the river breaks, and only a few scattered cliffs and an open cheat grass slope separated his crew from this fascinating river.

"Man, am I glad I couldn't see where we were going last night," Tony said as he looked back up the mountain. The mountain appeared to be straight up and down, with rock cliffs jutting up out of the brush. Blackened poles that had once been trees stood out from the ash-filled beds.

A heavy-set man with a shiny new short-wave radio hanging at his side moved slowly up the mountain toward the jumper crew. He was clean and his clothes were fresh, unlike the grubby, blackened figures of the jumpers. When he reached them he was gasping for breath and sweat soaked his shirt.

"Good job," he panted. "It's only a couple of hundred yards and you'll tie in with the crew working up from the bottom." He talked with Wayne for a few minutes, then continued his slow pace on up the fire line.

The sight of the men working up from the bottom brought new life to the worn-out jumpers and with renewed strength they started back to work.

The wind began to gust and Wayne said, "Jack, take Tony,

Guy, and Scott and give those folks some help. They are having trouble with a hot spot, and if it gets away from them we'll all be in trouble."

Scott was disappointed to hear that he would be working with Jack. They had been avoiding each other since the mosquito flip.

The men were halfway down to the lower crew when a violent wind swept up the mountain, tugging at Scott's shirt and knocking the hard hat from his head. It whipped the hot coals into flames that quickly leaped the line and raced up the mountain. Scott watched Jack, knowing that the red-head was the senior jumper and he was in charge. Jack poured water on his bandana. Gasping for air he prepared to press it to his face. The sight of Jack's distorted face suddenly triggered the rage that had smoldered in Scott since the mosquito flip. In his anger he again saw the cruel, snarling face with tobacco oozing from the lips! "The domineering BULLY! He is a fool! I won't trust him with *my* life!" Scott thought as his emotions burst the seams of his reason. With mucus pouring from his nose, his aching, tear-filled eyes peered into the boiling inferno. His throat was raw and pain stabbed at his lungs. "We can't waste any more time!" he choked from his parched lips. "I'm getting out of here!" Scott stood to start his panic-stricken plunge into the smoke.

"Stay down! STAY DOWN, SCOTT!" Jack commanded, chopping Scott's legs from under him with one stroke of his massive right arm.

With a crash Scott fell to the steep ground and rolled twice. The fall shocked him back to his senses and he realized that they had to stay together or no one would escape. They were in it together, Scott knew he would stay with the others if it cost him his life.

Sparks and ash rained down. Jack tried to sound calm, "We'll never out run it! Let's try to get to those rocks. Keep your shovels and canteens; we may have to dig in and let the fire burn over us," he choked.

Scott's heart pounded as he followed Jack's shadowy form. It was all he could do to keep from running blindly.

Jack again fell to the ground, and the others dropped beside him. With his face buried in the grass, Scott sucked air and dust into his burning lungs. "DIG! Dig as big a clearing as you can!" Jack ordered, slashing frantically with his shovel. There was no choice. Their only chance was to let the fire burn past them. Scott held his breath and desperately dug at the tough sod. No one spoke as the four grovelled for survival. A gust of wind drove the fire still closer, the flames scorching Scott's skin. His legs went weak. There was no escape. A helpless feeling came over him.

The scream of aircraft engines accelerating out of a dive was barely audible over the roar of the fire. "Is this a dream?" Scott questioned as the cool spray of chemical fire retardant rained down. It covered the four exhausted jumpers and the ground around them.

"Thank God!" Tony whispered, making the sign of the cross on his chest.

"That'll help," Jack's raspy voice said, "But it won't slow it down for long. Let's go, we've got to try to make the rocks."

They reached the rocks, and as they did, the wind died momentarily. "Don't stop! I think we can make it to the old burn," Jack panted.

"Let's go for it," Scott gasped, seeing that the rocks offered little protection. Mustering all his strength, Scott matched Jack, the college football star, stride for stride as they made a straight line through the heat of the briefly subsiding flames.

Scott looked back to see Guy bent over in a state of confusion. Scott was terrified! "I can't stand the heat and the smoke; I don't have strength enough to go back!" Scott was dizzy and fear sounded in his voice as he forced a gravelly h-o-o-t from his parched throat. Guy looked up and started toward them again.

The four blackened figures stood ankle deep in the ashes of the old burn, their eyes and lungs burning. The fire sped past them and up the mountain, sending a rolling wall of flame five feet into the air. They watched helplessly as the blaze hit the timber and raced through the tops of the trees. With a deafening roar, the flames reached twice as high as the trees as the fire torched into the midday sky. In a matter of minutes it destroyed the three miles of mountain side they had fought so hard to save. It was a terrifying sight even from the safety of the burned-over area.

Scott looked at Jack, relieved to be alive and grateful for his leadership. The haunting image of Jack during the "Mosquito Flip" was such a contrast to the colorless man before him. Jack's red hair and freckles were hidden under layers of soot and ash. His disarrayed clothes were riddled with burn holes, and his face was streaked from mucus and tears.

Scott felt ashamed and embarrassed by his breach of discipline. He would not accept his anger or panic for an excuse. He knew he had to make things right. "I... I... want to say I'm sorry

146

for nursing that grudge so long, and well... and... thanks for what you did today. Scott forced the words from his dry throat as sincerely as he had ever said anything.

"Maybe I should be apologizing to you, Scott," Jack answered quietly, still trying to get his breath. "I gave you a pretty good reason to hold a grudge; I carried the Ned business too far. I'm just glad we got it together when we needed to."

"Me too," Scott agreed, accepting Jack's outstretched hand.

"We may as well go to the bottom and see what's going on. We can't do any good here," Jack added.

"What about the others?" Scott asked, looking toward the raging flames where he had last seen Wayne and his crew.

"A fire would have trouble sneaking up on Wayne," Jack said, trying to be reassuring. "He has a lot of smarts about things like this." Yet Jack's face expressed concern as he started through the smoldering ruins toward the river.

Sprawled on the rocks they washed and rested, trying to get their bearings and decide on their next move. The fire continued to burn wildly in the premature dusk created by the heavy black overcast. Like an over-ripe egg yolk, the sun hung above the four weary men. They had to keep alert to avoid being hit by the rocks and burning logs that continually rolled out the bottom of the hellish mountain.

Jack eventually decided to take the trail that ran along the river and try to locate someone in charge. They were all eager to find out what had happened to Wayne and his crew.

Following the river for a mile, they came to the deserted tents that had been the fire camp. One man sat at a table with a large two-way radio in front of him. "Good to see you. I'll be amazed if we didn't burn some people up this time," he said between attempts to make radio contact with the various fire-fighting crews scattered across the face of the mountain.

"Have you heard from the jumpers on top?" Jack asked.

"Radio communication is bad. The only thing I'm sure of is that all our fire line has been lost and people are strung out all over," the radio operator answered. "We've got an order out for a thousand men and a regional overhead team. We'll be literally starting over on this one," he continued. "But no matter how many men we have, we can't do anything to slow this baby down until the weather gives us a break. You guys may as well find a shady spot and save your strength so you can fight again another day," he advised the jumpers.

"I can't rest when I don't know what kind of shape my friends are in," Jack said. All four jumpers paced around outside the operator's tent, moving close to listen each time the radio picked up a message.

"They're all right, I know they are," Scott told himself and the others.

"Yeah, that bunch can take care of themselves," they all agreed, as if agreement would make it so.

"Hey, Smokejumper," the radio man yelled over his shoulder.

"Ya," Jack responded as all four jumpers quickly surrounded the radio.

"I think I've got your friend on the radio now. Is his name Garrison?" the operator asked.

"Yes, that's him," Scott answered. "I knew they could make it if anyone could."

148

"Sure, I didn't doubt it for a minute," Jack added, now very confident.

The men crowded around the receiver. "Garrison to base camp! Garrison to base camp!" it crackled.

"This is base camp! I read you, Garrison! Go ahead!" the operator replied.

"Snap — s-n-a-p," the radio popped. "Eight jumpers OK. Eight jumpers are OK, crackle, snap...four smokejumpers missing...snap."

"I understand part of your message, Garrison. I think I know what you're asking. Four McCall smokejumpers safe at base camp. Repeat, four jumpers safe at base camp. Base camp over."

"Great!" came a fading reply through the static.

"They're all right!" Jack shouted joyfully.

Sprawled on sleeping bags around the deserted camp, the four managed to get a night's sleep. At daylight they awoke to the voices of Wayne and the other jumpers.

"Man, did you folks give us a scare!" Jack greeted Wayne. "I don't know how you got out of there yesterday."

"You think we can't take care of ourselves?' Wayne said, trying to joke off the near disaster. "We burrowed into a rock cliff, expecting to crawl out and gather up whatever was left of you four," Wayne continued. "Of course, we figured with Hardluck along, we might have some troubles ourselves!"

"Don't start it! Don't get on my case about this one!" Hardluck threatened. "We came closer to getting burned up than

I ever hope to again. That's serious and I don't want anyone to even jokingly blame me." Hardluck was angry and obviously hurt. The whole group fell silent.

For eight days the weary crews struggled with the treacherous fire, building a line at night and losing it in the winds of the hot afternoons. Then with the fire still uncontrolled, the McCall smokejumpers were recalled to their base. They were trucked to Salmon, Idaho, and later that same day they were flown to McCall, leaving other crews still battling the blaze.

Taking men off a fire that's burning out of control may seem strange to people unfamiliar with forest fire fighting procedures, but two planeloads of smokejumpers are missed very little on a thousand-man fire. The jumpers would be more efficiently used on the small fires that were expected from the predicted lightning storm.

The great blaze was called the "Corn Creek Fire" by Forest Service officials, and the "Corn Creek Disaster" by the McCall smokejumpers. It would continue to spread despite all efforts until the fall rains came. The Corn Creek Fire finally destroyed over thirty-five thousand acres of forest and watershed land and claimed several lives.

Hardluck was often teased and harassed about being bad luck, but his name was never again mentioned in connection with the Corn Creek Disaster.

18

SOMETHING IS WRONG

Scott was glad to be back to McCall after his long stay on the Corn Creek Fire. He was excited to see he had two letters from Julie and one from his folks. The frantic rotation of the jump roster slowed for a few days, and Scott had time to write some letters himself. So much had been happening.

The break was short lived, however, and it wasn't long before things were happening again. Scott's work detail returned one afternoon to find a group of jumpers standing outside the parachute loft. "What's going on?" Scott asked Jack.

"We dropped ten men today and another planeload is out now," Jack answered. "The whole camp is on stand-by."

"Here we go again," Scott said, tiredness in his voice. Yet he sensed something unfamiliar about the subdued group of men. They were not usually this quiet and inactive.

"What's this about a plane that is overdue?" Neil asked as he joined Scott and Jack.

"Oh, I don't think it is anything," Jack answered soberly.

"They haven't heard from the planeload of jumpers that Ken went out with this afternoon. That's not unusual, though."

"What do you mean, it isn't unusual?" Neil asked, still concerned.

"Sometimes in a thunderstorm like we're getting today, it's

hard to radio back in to McCall," Jack replied, pointing toward the dark clouds to the east. "The plane's radio may not be working, or sometimes the pilot would rather land and wait out a storm on a backwoods airstrip than have to return to McCall and then go back out with his load of jumpers. There are lots of things that can explain a delay in communication."

"People around here seem a little uptight," Jack added, "but I don't think there is anything to worry about."

This reasoning sounded good enough for Scott, and Neil seemed satisfied with it, too. Scott tried to ignore the uneasiness in his stomach. Neil walked over to another group of jumpers and was giving them Jack's explanation for the aircraft's not reporting in.

"B-u-z-z-z-z!" the alarm sounded. In a few short minutes, Scott was suited and in the plane as it climbed into the sky. "These fire calls are becoming familiar, but never routine," he thought as excitement filled his body. The plane proceeded north toward the Salmon River, which Scott had left behind only a few short days before.

"Hope it's not the Corn Creek Disaster," someone said, and the others groaned out in hardy agreement.

Guy leaned close to Scott's ear. "Hope nothing went wrong with the other plane," he said.

Scott tried to reassure Guy, "I'm sure nothing has. Jack says it's not uncommon not to hear from a plane for several hours at a time."

Scott was aware of the quiet in the jump plane, a very unusual situation in itself. The fast pace of the summer was beginning to show itself in the tired faces of those around him.

There was no joking or horseplay. The Twin Otter, too, seemed tired from the summer's toils as it plowed steadily across the mountains.

The fire was spotted. It seemed to be what Scott would now call a typical smokejumper fire. It was near the top of a ridge in an area with no roads. The fire covered about two acres.

The plane began circling the fire, and Don left his co-pilot seat and walked to the open door. Don was quiet, too. He seemed tired and he made no effort to talk with the men as he passed. He pulled on the emergency parachute and the communication headset. He drew three colored drift streamers from a box and began studying the fire as he directed the pilot over the spot he had chosen for the jump zone.

No one seemed enthusiastic about the job that lay ahead as they watched Don drop several sets of drift streamers. Scott secretly thought, "I hope it's too windy to jump. I don't feel like a tough night on the fire line. Something just isn't right."

Mechanically, the jumpers began adjusting equipment and preparing to exit the plane. In his turn Scott felt himself move through the ritual as those before him had done. He was tired. The strenuous summer had worn him down, and he felt the weight of a concern he didn't understand. His heart stopped momentarily when he caught the full blast of the open door.

"Something's not right! What's wrong?" Scott was ready to explode when he heard Don yell, "GO! GO!" and he flung himself out the door of the plane.

Then he was hanging beneath the bright orange and white canopy in the evening air. The roar of the plane grew more distant. Scott's eyes searched the area below for the small clearing. He hit the ground hard near the edge of the opening and rolled across some low-standing bushes.

Once on the ground, his concern and uneasiness persisted, and he sensed that the others shared this feeling. The smoke-jumpers quietly gathered in the clearing to prepare their attack on the fire. Chuck was in charge and he stood before the silent group. His eyes meeting theirs, he said, "Some of you have a pretty good idea of what I have to tell you." Chuck's raspy voice broke frequently revealing his pain. "I've waited until we were on the ground to tell you this because it wasn't confirmed until we were in flight. Telling you while we were in the plane just didn't seem to make sense." His strained voice became softer. "One of our jump planes has been missing all afternoon." Chuck's voice caught in his throat and he had to force out the words, "It crashed....." Then his voice stopped and tears ran slowly from his eyes.

Scott listened in disbelief, feeling dizzy as his breath seemed to hang up in his tight chest. "It isn't real. I won't believe what Chuck's saying," he thought to himself as he continued to listen.

"It was on the cargo drop," Chuck's strained voice went on. "All the smokejumpers were safely on the ground."

Scott felt a wave of relief moving through himself and the others, but then Chuck continued. "Ken was spotting and Jerry was the pilot. They didn't get out." Chuck's voice broke.

"Maybe the spotter got out! He wears a parachute and could have jumped at the last moment. Maybe they just haven't found him," Scott heard himself pleading.

"No," Chuck said with finality as he turned and picked up the chain saw that lay at his feet. He began walking toward the fire.

Scott felt the tears well up in his eyes and an ache tear at his insides. He worked at comprehending the nightmare the strange, raspy voice had spread before him in the growing darkness. "How could such a thing happen to Ken?" Scott questioned silently. "It can't be real. I thought Wayne's crew had gotten burned up on the Corn Creek Fire, but they hadn't. Maybe...? Somehow...? How does Chuck know...?" Doubt, confusion, and disbelief flooded Scott's mind. He was sick to his stomach and thought he was going to throw up.

The emotionally isolated crew slowly started to work the fire line. They worked silently, as they individually tried to deal with the pain Chuck's message had brought.

In the cold night air the fire showed no more spirit than the quiet firefighters and soon the feeble effort had the fire controlled.

Scott lay in his bedroll, looking at the stars as they dimmed into the dawn of the coming day. Slowly his sense of loss changed from shock to acceptance. The cold night air of late summer seemed to penetrate Scott's sleeping bag and chill his body.

Morning's light spread through the trees, revealing the clouds that had moved in during the night. It was a low, overcast sky. The sound of a light plane brought Scott fully awake. As it passed overhead he saw it drop a small package which fell momentarily and then blossomed into a white cargo chute with a bundle swinging beneath it.

Scott climbed out of his sleeping bag and moved toward the campfire. Near the fire Chuck opened the bundle and the delicious smell of hot breakfast poured from the insulated cartons. Included in the package was a copy of the Idaho Statesman newspaper. Its headlines read, "Boise School Counselor Dies in Plane Crash! Pilot Also Killed!" The paper was passed silently around the circle of smokejumpers as the breakfast lay untouched at their feet.

Scott glanced down the column. He read the description of the plane crash and swallowed hard to clear his throat. Then, turning quietly, he moved in silence to the edge of the clearing. The newspaper's account of how the low-flying plane had failed to pull out of the canyon where it was dropping cargo lingered painfully in Scott's mind. Nothing made sense to him now.

"All I know is that I'm tired," Scott thought. The tiredness penetrated the hollow center of his being. The lonely sickness pressed in on him as it seemed to kill his very will. "How can anything be important? Nothing matters. Nothing really matters but rest...I'm exhausted." Scott felt weak.

With little conversation, the day passed. The dispirited crew combed the fire for hot spots. The parachutes were taken down from the trees, and the equipment was placed where the ridge opened out above the river.

A light rain was falling as Scott and Guy made a tent out of a cargo chute, and crawled in to escape the wet darkness. Scott was dimly aware of the rain on the tent as his body seemed to spin and float off the ground. He let go and fell into an exhausted, fitful sleep.

The next morning Scott moved his body stiffly and reluctantly opened his eyes. The sides of the parachute tent had sagged and a long icicle hung down from the hole in the center. Scott could see his breath as he pulled on his cold, stiff clothes. Crawling out of the tent, he was unsettled by the strange, silent world around him. Nearly a half-inch of newly fallen snow lay on the ground. The forest was shrouded in white and fog lingered about the trees.

"Am I still asleep? Could this be a part of my dreams?" Scott asked himself as he moved to a viewpoint on the ridge. Fog filled the river bottom and clung to the mountainside. "What a mystical setting! A true setting for the stories Ken told me of the Indians and mountain men," Scott thought as he looked out on the snow-covered evergreens.

By the time the helicopter arrived in late afternoon, the sun had burned the fog away, and the late summer snow had disappeared into the ground. When it came time for Scott and Guy to load their gear in the side baskets of the helicopter and step from the landing skid into the clear bubble of the noisy machine, Scott was suddenly afraid. Helicopter rides had never scared him before, but now he caught his breath as they swung beneath the rotor blade and lifted above the trees. "How fragile life is..." Scott thought. "How quickly everything would end if the engine failed. The helicopter could hit a tree...get caught in a downdraft..." a hundred other possibilities flashed through his mind.

The romance of smokejumping was gone. "It's hard, dangerous work and that's all," Scott said to himself. He was tired and glad the fire season would soon be over. He needed time to think. "Is the risk worth it?" he asked himself.

19

SAYING GOOD-BYE TO

A FRIEND

The old DC-3 whined as the twin engines announced the arrival of a crosswind. There was no insulation or upholstery to stop the vibrations that ran through the thin fuselage like a cold chill. Scott stretched and looked at the men who sat facing each other on either side of the plane.

"Fellow travelers on this wilderness odyssey! What a summer we have shared!" Scott thought with a sigh.

Chuck was deep in thought as he leaned into the firewall just back of the cockpit. He looked unfamiliar, dressed in black slacks, oxfords and a white shirt open at the collar, revealing the scars on his neck. Ralph, "the Ned with the body of a pear," everyone's friend, sat with his eyes closed and his arms folded across his knit shirt. Mouse and Hardluck sat side by side, quiet for the first time all summer. Tony rested his elbows on his Levi covered knees. He cradled his chin in his hands as his fingers played nervously with his moustache. Neil, labeled "Pretty Boy" by Ken, read a paperback novel as the plane rocked above the primitive terrain. Tex was across from Neil. He wore a western shirt, Levis and his star-burst cowboy boots. Scott hadn't gotten

158

used to him without his walking cast.

Jack's normally fair complexion was weathered and his sun-burned nose was peeling. He was dressed much as he had been for the rodeo, the same pale blue western shirt with the small floral pattern. He also wore brown western cut pants and cowboy boots. "The rodeo!" Scott thought to himself. He smiled and shook his head as he looked at Jack and remembered the rodeo he almost rode in.

"Seems like years ago, doesn't it?" Jack said, acknowledging Scott's smile.

"Yep, it sure does," Scott answered, feeling good about Jack. "It sure does!"

Scott bumped Guy, who sat beside him, as he turned and looked out the window. The plastic window distorted Scott's view of the glacial meadows that appeared like scattered green islands in a sea of timbered mountains. His eyes focused on the man-made structure reaching skyward from one of the highest peaks. The sight of the lookout tower triggered a flood of emotion in Scott. "Sheepeater Lookout," Scott said under his breath. He felt the wetness build in the corners of his eyes as he remembered the night by the glowing campfire when Ken told him the Sheepeater story. He thought of how the Sheepeaters valued their freedom, and of Ken with his quick smile and his courage to meet life head on. He remembered Ken telling of the rituals that marked a young Sheepeater's passage into the adult world. Scott felt that Ken shared something with these historic people, and he shared something with Ken. Scott didn't understand. And he knew no words to express his feelings.

Scott saw Chamberlain Basin to the front and left of the

plane.

"It's beautiful country! I can see why Ken's wife chose this spot," Guy said as the plane started its circling glide toward the small clearing.

"It's the heart of Idaho's Primitive Area," Scott said. "Ken loved it."

The DC-3 touched down and came to a stop just a few feet short of the trees; then it taxied to where several small planes were parked.

The smokejumpers unloaded from the plane and joined the others as they gathered near a pine tree just off the runway. Scott's eyes followed the beautiful timbered skyline as the minister began the service with the words of Richard Allen:

As you face your death,
It is only the love
You have given
And received
Which will count.
If you have loved well
Then it will have been worth it
But if you have not
Death will always come too soon
And be too terrible to face.

Scott knew that Ken had loved well and lived life to its fullest. If Ken could have added to Richard Allen's words he might have said:

Don't feel sorry for the man who dies young,
But save your sorrow for the man
Who directs his life from a position of fear

160

And hasn't the courage to meet life and live it.

Scott's mind was clear. The long searching days since the plane crash had left him with a calmness he had never experienced. He now realized that death was as much a part of life as birth. Scott could sense the spirit of the Sheepeaters and he felt a closeness to those around him. "I am a part of all people, through all time," Scott thought as he recognized the meaning of the serenity he had found. He had changed. This had been the summer of Scott's "Vision Quest." Like the youth of the Sheepeater tribe, he had been visited by the Atutelary Spirit and received the song for his life.

Scott's senses were flooded with the Idaho wilderness as he thought, "I choose not to hide from life. I will smokejump for many summers to come, treading the trails of the mountain men and passing through the hallowed homeland of the Sheepeaters. The friendship I've shared with Ken is my ever present link with their courageous drive to live free."

About the Author

Dale L. Schmaljohn, Ed. D., is a native of Idaho. He was a smokejumper based in McCall, Idaho for eleven summers and trained new smokejumpers for five seasons. He has traveled over much of the western United States, parachuting and fighting forest fires in inaccessible mountain areas.

Dr. Schmaljohn is currently a licensed psychologist, specializing in child and educational psychology.